# A Dog for
# CHRISTMAS

## AN AMISH CHRISTMAS ROMANCE

# LINDA BYLER

Good Books

New York, New York

A DOG FOR CHRISTMAS

Good Books books may be purchased in bulk at special discounts for sales promotion, corporate gifts, fund-raising, or educational purposes. Special editions can also be created to specifications. For details, contact the Special Sales Department, Good Books, 307 West 36th Street, 11th Floor, New York, NY 10018 or info@skyhorsepublishing.com.

Good Books is an imprint of Skyhorse Publishing, Inc.®, a Delaware corporation.

Visit our website at www.goodbooks.com.

10 9 8 7 6 5 4 3 2 1

Library of Congress Cataloging-in-Publication Data is available on file.

ISBN: 978-1-68099-760-6
eBook ISBN: 978-1-68099-334-9

Cover design by Koechel Peterson & Associates, Inc.

Printed in the United States of America

# Table of Contents

# Chapter One

HENRY AND HARVEY WERE BORN ON A COLD January night, just before the blizzard of 1929.

Their mother laid them next to her, side by side in the double bed, wondering how they would manage to feed nine children when times were lean.

By the time the twins were six years old, she had borne four more babies, bringing the total to thirteen children. They managed from year to year until 1936, when the lean times became leaner still. Oatmeal gave way to cornmeal mush, ground from the leftover field corn and roasted in the oven of the Pioneer Maid wood range.

Rueben Esh, the children's father, worked the farm from morning till evening. Tall, thin, and just a bit weary, his brown eyes questioned why milk prices were so low. With thirteen children to feed, his mortgage payment was increasingly hard to meet.

Savilla, the good wife, spare and angular, patched their clothes and pinched pennies, cooked green beans and potatoes without a smidgen of meat, sold eggs and butter, and rode into the town of Intercourse, Pennsylvania, on the spring wagon, with half a dozen brown-eyed children who never in their lives ate an egg for breakfast.

Much too wasteful, to let a child eat an egg, when they could bring the wonderful price of a dollar a dozen.

Milk fever set in after the birth of the fourteenth child, and Savilla died.

The twins were seven years old, their unruly brown hair bouncing above button noses splattered with freckles, their brown eyes not quite aligned. When they looked at you, they saw not only you, but what was behind you as well.

They pressed around their mother's coffin, swallowing their tears, standing side by side in their grief, the way they'd lain side by side in the double bed at birth.

They knew hunger and cold and filth, that next year. The oldest daughter was overcome with the avalanche of responsibilities. She sat and rocked Baby

Ezra while the rest of them did the best they could, under the tutelage of their sad-eyed father.

When he married Mattie Stoltzfus, she entered the house like a freight train, tall and wide and hissing steam. The twins sat wide-eyed on the worn-out davenport that smelled of cow manure and sour milk, and wondered how they'd manage in times like this.

They knew they disliked Mattie, so they agreed that they wouldn't do what they were told. They never spoke back to her, just stood and looked at her with their curiously unfocused gaze and disobeyed.

Rueben Esh listened to his new wife, found a green willow branch, and switched their thin bottoms, his sad brown eyes filled with resolve.

"She doesn't like us," Harvey said.

"No, she doesn't," Henry said.

The parents made arrangements, packed their clothes into two brown paper sacks, and sent them down the road to neighbors who had only three children of their own.

Rueben stayed in the barn that day, left the parting to Mattie.

December 18, a week before Christmas, they stepped off the porch in their torn shoes into a few inches of snow, through the wire gate and out the lane, past the barnyard and the bare maple trees that waved their black branches in the cold wind.

The boys didn't look back, knowing that what was behind them was something they could never have again.

After the first mile, their feet were cold from snow leaking into the cracks in the soles of their shoes. Their hands were red and chapped from the cold, so they switched their paper sacks from one hand to the other. Their torn straw hats flapped in the wind, and occasionally they took a free hand to slap the top of it. Behind them, their tracks zigzagged through the frozen pellets of snow, but they never strayed from each other, their shoulders meeting again and again.

A buggy passed from the opposite direction. They waved solemnly and kept walking. They were being sent to Ephraim King. They had been told how far to walk on Peters Road, where to turn, and which drive-way to look for, so they recognized the place when they came to it. A low rise, and suddenly, behind the woods, there it was.

Instinctively, they drew together. Their steps slowed. The wind blew cold. They could hear their stomachs rumble underneath their thin coats that closed down the front with hooks and eyes.

The farm where they were expected to live looked much the same as any other Lancaster County farm. A white-sided house with a porch and a *kesslehaus*, a white barn with white outbuildings flanked by patches of woods and corn-stubbled fields, a winding creek with willow trees swaying bare-limbed on its border.

"I guess they know we're coming."

"I hope so."

Unsure which door to enter, they hesitated at the end of the cement sidewalk. No barking dogs announced their arrival, no one appeared at a window, and both doors stayed shut, as if the farmhouse had turned its face aside.

They looked at each other, one's uncertainty mirrored in the other's brown eyes.

"You want to go back?"

"We can't."

Harvey nodded, and together they moved to the front door, lifted their fists, and knocked, first one, then the other.

A patter of feet, and the door opened.

"Oh, it's you! I was watching for you. Thought your *dat* would bring you *mit die fuhr*. Have you walked all this way?"

"Yes."

She opened the door wider, standing aside to usher them in. She was of medium height, and not too thin. On her round face, spectacles perched on her wide nose. Light-colored eyes peered through the polished lenses, her small red mouth like a raspberry. They noticed the row of safety pins down her dress front and the narrow gray apron belt with a row of small pleats across her stomach. The apron was wet, as if she had left her dishwater. She extended not one, but two, warm hands, red from the hot water.

"Well, here you are, then. We are looking forward to having you. My name is Rachel. But I suppose now I am your Mam. You may call me Mam. We have three girls, Malinda, Katie, and Anna. They are in school. They will be home this afternoon.

You are Henry and Harvey Esh, right?"

"I'm Henry."

"I'm Harvey."

She rolled her eyes, raised her hands, and laughed, a long rolling sound that neither of them had heard very much in their short lives. They didn't smile, only watched Rachel with a serious, off-kilter expression in their brown eyes, unsure if they were being mocked or merely laughed at in a kind way.

"I'll never know which is which. Well, what does it matter. Here, give me your bags. I believe we have the necessary clothes in here, right?"

They both nodded.

Four eyes looked at her, two of them not quite focused with the others. Rachel stepped closer, peered into their faces.

"Your eyes. . ."

She straightened, led them to the *kesslehaus*, and showed them where to keep their shoes and hang their coats and hats.

The *kesslehaus* was warm with the steam coming from the *elsa-Kessle*, the great kettle built into the brick oven, with a heavy cast iron door in front, where wood was shoved through to heat the water above it. There was a white Maytag wringer washer with a galvanized tub for rinsing, a painted gray chest, a sink built into cupboards, and a cream separator in the corner by a door. The cement floor was painted gray, slick and shining.

After Rachel took their paper sacks and set them in a corner, she turned to them with a serious expression.

"Now, I will have to check your heads for lice."

Willingly, they bowed their heads as she took them to the white light by a window and lifted their wavy brown hair, peering closely behind their scabby ears.

She said nothing, just took them to the *kesslehaus* and doused their heads well with coal oil, then lifted a bucket of steaming water, added lava soap, and scoured their heads. Retrieving a galvanized tub, she made them bathe all over.

She pinned their heads to her stomach and washed their ears and the sides of their necks, taught them how to use a toothbrush and baking soda, then told them to sit at the table and she'd get their dinner.

They felt pink and scrubbed. They wiggled their toes inside their patched socks, touched their raw scalps, and watched Rachel with solemn eyes.

She had dimples in her elbows that only appeared when her arms hung straight down. Her covering was not as big as Mattie's. Her hair was rolled tight on each side of her head, and her dress was navy blue.

She was making something in a pan that she stirred all the time. It smelled sweet, like cornstarch pudding.

Their mouths watered. They swallowed.

Harvey wiped away a trickle of saliva.

Henry was dizzy with hunger.

Mattie had not given them breakfast, saying the cornmeal was low. But now, past dinnertime, the thin reserve they had was almost used up.

Harvey felt hollow inside, like the bottom of tall grass in the fall when it turned brown. Henry thought he might fall off his chair if he couldn't get the kitchen to stop spinning.

Rachel got down a tin of saltines, spread them with butter, then ladled a thick, yellow pudding over them.

"Do you like crackas and cornstarch?"

"We don't know."

"You never had it?"

"No."

"All right."

That was all she said, then left them alone.

Harvey looked at Henry.

Henry nodded.

They bowed their heads, their hands clasped in their laps. Too shook up to pray, they waited till the proper time to lift their heads, then took up their spoons and ate the sweetened pudding and the salty, buttery saltines that melted on their tongues.

They scraped their plates, and sat, unsure what they should do now.

Rachel appeared, asked if they wanted more.

They nodded, quickly.

She refilled their plates, and they ate until they scraped their bowls a second time. A full stomach was a new sensation, and with the scrubbing with soap and hot water, their eyelids fell heavily. They made their way to the couch by the windows, and fell asleep in bright light of the afternoon sun on the snow.

When the girls came home from school, swinging their black lunch buckets, they stopped inside the *kesslehaus* door when their mother appeared with lowered brows and a finger held to her lips.

"*Die boova sinn do.*"

Carefully, the girls tiptoed to hang up their bonnets, hiding their faces for a few seconds longer than they normally would have.

Malinda, the oldest, was the first to turn, questioning her mother with her small blue eyes.

"Why are they sleeping?" she whispered.

Harvey woke up first, blinked, then sat up quickly, his hair tousled and stiff from the kerosene wash.

Henry followed, clearly ashamed to be caught napping, rubbed his eyes and slid a glance sideways at Harvey, gauging the mood of his brother. He sidled closer, until their shoulders touched.

Katie stood by the rocking chair, small, round and blue-eyed, dressed in a purple dress and black pinafore-style apron, her hair rolled back like ropes, sleek and glistening, her face an open book, revealing eagerness and curiosity, like a squirrel.

The boys gazed back at her, four brown eyes that took in every detail of this girl they would supposedly call their sister.

Anna wasn't interested. She went upstairs, like a wisp of fog that blew through the room and that no one was absolutely sure had been there at all.

Malinda, prodded by her mother, walked over and peered at them, tall, thin, a black apron pinned around her skinny waist with safety pins, her green dress buttoned down the back with small green buttons. She wore black stockings and the biggest black shoes the boys had ever seen, coming up over her ankles, tied with black laces in a row of holes that marched up her foot like ladybugs.

The reason Henry noticed her shoes was because he lowered his face and kept it lowered when Malinda approached.

"Hello."

She stuck out a hand for the traditional Amish handshake.

Henry took it, then Harvey did, but cautiously.

"So you will be my new brothers?"

Two sets of shoulders were shrugged, first one, then the other.

"Can't you talk?"

Two heads nodded.

"What's wrong with your eyes?"

And that was the twins' introduction to a new life in a strange house, doing chores in an unaccustomed barn with a new father who did not resemble their own in the least.

Ephraim King was of medium height, built like a bulldog, massive shoulders and neck, large hands with fingers like knobby branches, legs that bowed out from the knees, so that when he walked his steps looked like a broken pair of scissors.

He was loud, and always talking, or whistling, and sometimes he broke into song, snatches of hymns, but most often, silly little songs that made no sense.

> The bear went over the mountain,
>
> The bear went over the mountain,
>
> The bear went over the mountain,
>
> To see what he could see.

That was one. There were many more, so the twins found themselves creeping through the barn, hoping to catch another song. But too often it wasn't worth their tiptoeing, when he was only whistling.

He was always happy, that was one thing sure.

The first few days, Ephraim's happiness carried the boys along, acquainting them to their altered existence. It was all so befuddling, a new bedroom upstairs, the stairway cut in half by a landing, then veering off to the left to continue on its way.

Sent to bed without a light, they both ran into the wall before learning the stairway turned to the left.

In the mornings, they were expected to rise in the stark, frigid air of the strange room, dress and be downstairs at 5:30, walk through the kitchen to the *kesslehaus*, shivers waving over their backs and down their legs, dress in their chore boots and coats by the light of a blue kerosene lantern, already lit and set on the countertop of the sink.

Their appearance inside the warm barn, moist and steaming with the Holsteins' breathing, always brought a cheerful "*Guta Marya, boova.*"

They were expected to answer in the same way, so they did, hesitantly at first. This whole *Guta Marya* thing was so brand new and out of the ordinary, they only mumbled the words in a hoarse whisper.

There were calves to be fed, heifers to give forkfuls of hay, which proved to be more than they could handle. They stood side by side in the dark, frosted morning, when the east was changing from night to a gray awakening that would turn to a splash of lavender and pink, and pondered the problem of the lengthy pitchfork handle, the amount of hay to be moved, and the allotted time they were given to accomplish this.

"Wheelbarrow's too slippy in the snow," Harvey said.

"Wagon's too small," Henry said. "Think the man would get us a tarp to fork the hay on, slide it down?"

"Don't know. We can ask."

They had a hard time calling him Dat. There was only one Dat, and that was Rueben Esh, tall, thin as a stovepipe, sad-eyed and quiet as a forest pool on a still day.

They could not place noisy, whistling, smiley-faced Ephraim in the notch reserved for Rueben.

So they compromised and called him *da mon*.

They didn't understand the tooth brushing, either. All that effort, ramming a toothbrush back and forth, upside down and inside out, with that vile tasting white baking soda on it, just did not seem necessary.

Malinda showed them how to wet the bristles of the toothbrush and hold it in the dish of baking soda. It didn't make it easier.

Another perplexing thing was all the food being carried into the house. How could one family eat so much food?

Harvey asked Henry that night, snuggled together in the big double bed, warm and cozy on the soft flannel sheets that smelled like some flower they couldn't name. The covers on top of their thin bodies were so heavy and warm, they could easily feel as if The Good Man who lived in Heaven had his Hand pressed down at the quilts and sheep's-wool comforter.

It felt so good, to be warm from the top of their kerosene tainted head to their skinny pink toes.

"Why do you think they went away with their buggy and came back with all those paper sacks?" he asked, his voice burry with sleep.

"It has to do with Christmas," Henry answered, yawning.

"Oh."

Then, "Christmas at home wasn't different from any other day, was it?"

"Sometimes we had a *Grischtag Essa* at Doddy Beiler's. Remember we got an orange? It was so sour I fed mine to the chickens. Mam pinched me and twisted my ear."

"Ow," Harvey said, levelly.

"Guess I should have eaten it myself."

"Probably would have been best."

"I miss my mam, sort of."

"I miss her. Dat too."

"You think they think of us?"

"Yes. But they can't afford us."

"I know."

Their breathing slowed and deepened. Their little chests rose and fell underneath all those covers, their forms making barely a bump that anyone could see.

The brown pupils of their eyes disappeared beneath the heavy lids that slid over them, as thick, black lashes, like teeth on a comb, lay on their thin cheeks.

A shaft of moonlight found its way beneath the green pulldown shade, creating a patch of light on the heavy rag rug beside the bed. The walnut chest of drawers with porcelain knobs stood guard against the opposite wall, the glass berry set from Ephraim's mother resting on the oval embroidered dresser scarf.

The floor was polished pine wood, smooth and clean in the moonlight. Their only possessions were hung in the closet, behind the door with a white glass knob, the paper sacks folded and stored beneath a can seated on a chair in the corner.

Outside, a heavy, sugary snow lay over the forests and harvested fields of Lancaster County. Roads crisscrossed the landscape like etchings in a pie crust, punctured by dark ponds and waterways not yet frozen, the dark icy water gobbling up the crystalized snowflakes as they fell.

The horses in the tie stalls rested their weight on two legs and fell asleep as the winter's cold deepened. Cows rattled their chains, harrumphing a loud exhalation of breath as their legs folded clumsily beneath them, their massive weight settling around them as they dozed. The hens in the henhouse tucked their pointed beaks under their wings, the straw beneath them soiled with broken egg yolk.

The covered bridge that spanned Pequea Creek snapped and groaned as the moist cold settled into the impressive timbers used in its construction. Below, the icy black waters flowed, swift, deep, and menacing.

Till morning there was an embroidery of thin ice lining the banks, where the water swirled and eddied in silent pools, downstream from overgrown tree roots. Large bass and carp lay dormant, their metabolism slowed to conserve energy, their colors blending with the light and shadow that played on the creek bed. Beneath the silt and mud, frogs and turtles were burrowed, spending the winter months away from the freezing temperatures, to begin the cycle of life all over again in the spring.

Life slowed and hummed around Henry and Harvey as they slept the deep sweet slumber of children.

Displaced, innocent, accepting their lot in life without complaint, they lay side by side, the way they had been placed at birth, without knowing what their life would bring, as children do. Already, they had placed their trust in Ephraim and Rachel, to feed them and keep them warm, the only two things they would need.

Those three girls would just have to learn to like them, being as unimpressed as they were.

Nothing to be done about that.

# Chapter Two

THE TWINS WATCHED IN WIDE-EYED WONDER the goings-on in their new home.

Mam, as she was to be called but still thought of as Rachel by both of them, was a flurry of activity sending the girls off to school amid stern warnings: find their own boots and mittens, and no, she hadn't seen a package of pencils, but if they'd learn to keep track of their things they wouldn't have to go through this, finished with a screech about looking at the clock and don't they see what time it is.

Her face was red, her hair frizzy, and her covering sideways as she whirled from room to room with a dustrag, a wet mop, and a bucket with hot, soapy water.

Henry was secretly glad that Rachel told off Malinda; she was only ten, but she acted as if she was as old as her mother, which she wasn't, so he figured it was time she found out.

Teeth brushing and face washing were two of her forms of torture, so if she wasn't put in her place, hard telling what else she'd come up with. But of course, they said nothing, just sat quietly side by side and watched with their slightly unfocused gaze.

Ephraim King thought it would be best to keep the boys at home from school for a week, let them become acquainted with their new surroundings before being introduced back to the schoolhouse in Leacock Township, a large brick building that housed forty pupils and had one teacher. The children were mostly English, and they had an English teacher named Mrs. Dayble.

She was tall and wide and as mean as a *gluck* on her nest. She terrified Henry and Harvey both.

But it was school, and they knew they had to go. They watched their p's and q's, finished their work on time, and watched the teacher with their dark eyes, knowing where she was at every moment. They knew her pinching was painful, so they didn't plan on having their palms rapped with the sharp side of a wooden ruler.

They had watched Benjamin Stoltzfus standing by the privy with his hands in his pockets, blinking back tears of pain, after a few cracks with that ruler.

They sat up and took notice of any behavior that was unacceptable.

Rachel's sister Lydia showed up that morning. Short and round, her apron flaring from her hips, she sailed into the house in a cloud of cheer and good-will, to help *die schveshta* Rachel get ready for the family Christmas dinner.

The family included ten siblings, a mother and father (on the Beiler side), and somewhere between sixty and seventy children. They weren't exactly sure.

Amos and Annie had a new one, little Emma, who was their sixth girl and no boys. They thought Davey and Fannie's little one was already six weeks old, so that made nine for them. Another boy. Was it Manasses or Ephraim? Ephraim, they believed. He was a big one, weighing over ten pounds.

Well, no wonder. Fannie was a chunk herself, so what did she expect, eating all that bread? Ei-ya-yi.

Henry and Harvey were sent to the barn to help Ephraim, so they donned their denim coats, pursing their lips in concentration as they bent their heads to close the hooks and eyes down the front. They sat on the painted cement floor and tugged on the rubber Tingley boots, smashed their tattered straw hats on their heads, and slipped and slid their way to the barn to find him.

"Ephraim," Henry said.

"Dat," Harvey corrected.

"Dat," Henry agreed.

When they found him, he smiled, leaned on his pitchfork, and asked what they were up to.

"We're supposed to help you."

"Rachel sent you out?"

They nodded, together.

"All right. You can sweep cobwebs in the forebay. *Schpinna hoodla* all over the walls. I'll get the ceiling."

So they obeyed, found brooms, and began to sweep the walls. Their brooms were meshed with the spiderwebs in a short time, and their arms became tired long before they were finished. But they kept on working, eager to please Ephraim. Over and over they swept between the sturdy brown timbers that held up the walls of the barn, until there wasn't a spiderweb to be found.

Ephraim came to check on their progress, and smiled. He hooked his thumbs in his trouser pockets, lifted his face to the walls, and gave a low whistle.

"*Gute boova! Fliesichy boova.* You did a good job. Now we want to clean the *vassa droke.*"

He showed them what he wanted done—the water carried out in buckets and dumped beside the barnyard fence.

With the high praise ringing in their ears, they lifted buckets of dirty water, riddled with hay and grain and the horses' saliva, straining to carry each one through the door of the barn, across the slippery, packed-down snow to dump it in the low place by the fence, as they had been instructed.

The cold water sloshed across their trouser legs and darkened the fronts of their coats. Their hands turned purplish red. Their mouths compressed with determination, they scurried in and out of the forebay, like two straw-hatted ants, intent on receiving more high praise from their new father.

They scrubbed and scrubbed the sides and bottom of the cast iron watering trough, pebbled and rough, green slime and bits of hay loosening as they worked.

Their stomachs growled with hunger. Slower and slower they wielded the wooden, stiff-bristled scrubbing brushes. Just when they were beginning to wonder if Ephraim had forgotten them, he appeared at the door.

"*Boova, Kommet. Vella essa.*"

He didn't inspect their work, neither did he praise them, so they walked to the house, their heads bent, sober and confused. Had they dumped the water in the wrong place? Was the scrubbing done all wrong?

Henry told Harvey not to worry that he had not checked their work; he would do that later.

They had both been thinking the same thing, and this comforted Harvey, nodding his head eagerly.

The smell of cooking greeted them in the *kesslehaus*, steam rising upward from beneath the metal lid of the "*elsa Kessle*," creating a moist heat that felt wonderful as they shrugged out of their coats and hung them on hooks, slapped their straw hats on top, and bent to wriggle their shoes out of the rubber boots. They took turns washing their hands and faces with the green, gritty, and strong-smelling bar of Lava soap. They dried themselves on the navy-blue roller towel, running a hand through their wavy brown hair, and went to the kitchen.

The kitchen was fragrant with heat and spices. The overpowering smell, sweet and delicious, caused both boys to swallow as saliva rose in their mouths.

They couldn't look at the rows of cookies cooling on the countertop. They had never imagined such a sight. Dark brown molasses cookies sprinkled with white sugar, pale sugar cookies with pink frosting, chocolate cookies that were small and shaped like bells, squares of brown cookies with walnut halves pressed into them.

This was only seen with stolen glances. Harvey lifted his waterglass and drank. Henry did too. They sat back and listened to the grownups, talking about the weather and if there'd be more snow for Christmas.

Was Amos busy?

Oh, he was just *hesslich hinna-noch*. He had spent too much time with the corn husking, now he still had the fodder to gather, which he wasn't going to get done in the snow. Not now anymore.

But she didn't mean to *glauk*, he worked too hard; what they really needed was a good *knecht*.

Ephraim nodded and smiled, his small blue eyes twinkling in his wide face, his brown beard bushy, surrounding his face like the bristles of a soft broom, hanging below his chin in stiff waves.

"I have two of them now," he said, turning to the twins. "*Ach, ya. Die glany boovy.*"

Lydia flushed with pleasure as she eyed them both, her face lined with more smiles as she spoke. Rachel placed a steaming dish of chicken potpie in the middle of the table, followed by one of mashed sweet potatoes mounded high, a river of browned butter dripping down the sides. There was applesauce in a glass dish, pickled red beets, small green cucumbers in another, and slabs of homemade cheese layered on a blue platter, pale golden with perfectly round holes in every slice.

Lydia and Rachel kept talking and Ephraim kept listening. They were discussing the runaway team of horses over toward *Nei Hullant.*

Finally, Ephraim cleared his throat and stayed quiet, which was the signal for the women to finish talking, bow their heads, fold their hands in their laps, and pray silently before they ate.

The boys' plates were filled with heavy, thick squares of potpie swimming with chunks of chicken, carrots, celery, and onion in a smooth golden gravy. The sweet potatoes in browned butter weren't as good, but they ate the mound that was put on their plates.

The cheese was good too, sprinkled with salt and eaten with the little green sweet pickles.

They sat quietly, their stomachs pleasantly stretched, the warmth of the kitchen coloring their cheeks to a red glow.

They kept stealing glances at the cookies but said nothing. Rachel served cups of steaming peppermint tea, followed by the sugar bowl.

"Just one spoonful," she told the boys.

They dipped their heads, embarrassed now, as if their new mother had known they'd planned on using two or three if that sugar bowl was passed with the tea.

They never had sugar in their tea at home.

And then, like a miracle, she got up and began piling cookies on a dinner plate. Every kind.

"Cookies!" Ephraim said, laughing.

Harvey chose a chocolate one. Henry slowly lifted a sugared molasses cookie, watching the grown-ups' faces for signs of disapproval.

"Surely you want more than one," Ephraim called out. "It's Christmastime. You may try as many cookies as you want."

"Go ahead, boys," Rachel urged.

So they did. They tasted every different kind of cookie. It was amazing what happened to a mouthful of cookie crumbs if you drank tea. Everything melted and blended in with the tea until there was nothing left but a whole mouthful of unbelievable sweetness to swallow. Then you could bite off another bit of cookie and start all over again.

The grown-ups kept talking, so the twins kept eating cookies. The kitchen swam as their eyelids became heavy with the warmth in the room, their full stomachs, and the strenuous work they had done.

But when they got back to the barn to begin their vigorous scrubbing, they felt wonderful. Full of energy, happier than they had been since the day they arrived.

"I think we have a good home," Harvey said.

"I believe we do," Henry agreed solemnly.

"The Good Man must have heard our *Müde bin-nich*."

"I believe so."

When Ephraim came to tell them their mother wanted them in the house, they laid down their brushes and watched his face for signs of approval.

"Good job, boys. Well done."

Words as sweet as peppermint tea and cookies. Words they had never heard before from the sad-eyed father to whom they had been born.

For a long time after that Christmas, the boys would always look at the sparkling clean water in the cast iron trough, remember all over again how they had done well, the thought lifting their small shoulders and straightening their knobby spines, giving them a spring in their step and a fierce, undying devotion to Ephraim King.

It was the same with Rachel.

The reason she called them in was to introduce them to gingerbread men. Christmas was not complete without children making gingerbread men, and with the family Christmas gathering at their house, she would not have time to allow the girls to help after school.

So the boys got the job.

They concentrated, bit their tongues and crossed their eyes, and tried so hard to cut out perfect gingerbread men. They placed the raisins in the exact position, even became silly and turned the raisins down instead of up, to form a frowning gingerbread man.

Whey Lydia and Rachel threw up their hands and laughed with them, they giggled and made a few more. They watched them come from the oven, puffed up and spicy, and when they were told to try one, they passed the hot gingerbread man from hand to hand to cool it, before biting off the top of the head, being careful to watch Rachel's face for a sign that they were doing something wrong.

When the girls came home from school, there was a general upheaval as they examined the cookies and fussed about the gingerbread men.

Malinda ate a frowny-faced one, then pretended to be in a bad mood, the cookie having the power to do that. Harvey thought she was serious, his eyes turning bright with shame and unshed tears. Henry became very quiet and sober.

Anna said she was only joking, but it took a while till the boys trusted Malinda and returned to their usual selves.

Katie said they couldn't have done better.

It was almost too much, all this approval. Harvey was not sure it should be this way, and told Henry so.

"I mean, surely soon, something bad will happen. We'll do something wrong, like break a glass or a plate, and then will everything will be as usual."

"Our mam was not mean. Just tired, with too many children."

"Yes. Too many. We were too many children. There were two of us at one time, so we were too many."

They pondered the truth for a few minutes.

"I think Mattie probably misses us. She liked us, all right."

"Yes. Yes, she did."

So they repeatedly assured themselves that it was the fact that they had too many children that they were sent away. Then Harvey declared their own Savilla mother would not have sent them to live with

Ephraim King. It didn't matter how many children she had.

"She died, so she doesn't know," Henry said.

"Maybe she does."

"Naw. She's dead. You don't know anything if you're dead."

"If you go to Heaven and become an angel, you do."

"But not to look down here."

"You don't know."

"You don't, either."

"Nobody does."

They solemnly accepted this bit of wisdom together.

They pushed heavy coarse bristled brooms across the rough cement of the forebay. At one time, the concrete floor had been smooth, but with the iron shod hooves of countless horses clattering over it, the surface became pitted. So they pushed the broom, over and over across the same area, until there was no dust or bits of straw and hay.

After that, they were allowed to go sledding in the back pasture. Ephraim produced a long wooden sled with steel runners and a bar across the front that you could push or pull on either side to turn the sled to the left or right. A rope was attached to holes drilled on each side, long enough so you could pull it behind you comfortably.

The sun shone in a cloudless blue sky, the cold was tinged with a bit of warmth in the afternoon, the white slopes stretched before them like a brilliant promise.

They talked and laughed, jerked the sled along as they leaped joyous little bounces of energy, slipped and slid up the hill until they reached the top. It felt like a mountain. They could see wedges of dark forest thrusting into the white corn-stubbled fields, the neighboring farms nestled like toys between them. Roads zigzagged through the snowy countryside, an occasional gray buggy pulled by a trotting horse moved along at a snail's pace.

Harvey laid the rope carefully along the surface of the sled. He looked at Henry.

"Lie down or sit?"

Henry eyed the long descent, pursed his lips with the decision.

"Better lie down."

So Harvey flung himself on the sled, with Henry coming down hard on top of him.

"Don't hit the fence at the bottom," he yelled in Harvey's ear as the sled began a slow coast in the sugary snow. Speed picked up rapidly. The wind brushed their faces with cold. Yelling their exhilaration, they reached up to smooth their straw hats down on their heads, but it did no good. Halfway down the long slope, the wind grabbed the hats and flung them away, to skitter across the snow, rolling like a plate.

Then there was only the heart-stopping speed, the cold rush of air that brought tears to their eyes, making a white blur of everything. The sled's runners made no sound; their ears filled with air and their own shouts.

Harvey leaned on the right side of the wooden rudder, desperately trying to avoid the oncoming fence. They escaped by inches, rolling off the sled at the last instant, sprawled in the snow, their bodies convulsed in helpless giggles.

"Hu-uh!" Henry finished.

"Whoo-eee!" Harvey echoed, pounding the snow with his bare fists.

They leaped to their feet, stuck one cold reddened hand into one pocket of their trousers, bent over and ran back up the hill, their noses running, their faces wet with spitting snow.

"Hey!" Harvey pointed.

Together, they watched a huge, lolloping dog stop to inspect a straw hat, look in their direction before grabbing the brim in his teeth, lifting his head with the treasure he found, and running across the slope.

They took off after him, dropped the rope, and the sled careened haphazardly down the hill, to rest against a fence post.

"Dog! Dog! Stop!"

They ran, shouted, slipped and slid to their knees, jumped up, and resumed the chase. The huge dog stopped, turned, eyed them, but kept the straw hat clutched in his mouth. Dipping his head, he wheeled away with the odd gallop of a big, ungainly dog.

Out of breath, their legs shaking with fatigue, the boys stopped. They looked at each other.

"Whose dog?" they both said at once.

They both shrugged their shoulders and resumed their running. The dog stopped. He dropped the hat, his mouth wide, his tongue lolling, and watched the boys approach. His tail began to wag like a flag waving. As they neared, he bent his front legs, leaped to the side, took up the hat, and bounded away, looking back over his shoulder to taunt them.

They were going farther and farther away from their farm. Woods rose up in front of them, a tangle of briars and tall weeds growing around the trunks of huge trees, their leaves gone, with branches spread to the sky like a giant pattern.

The boys stopped. The only sound was their ragged breathing. The dog stopped, the hat in his mouth. He wagged his long, bushy tail in surrender, sat down and dropped the hat, his mouth spread like a welcoming smile.

Henry extended a hand, wiggling his fingers.

"Here, dog. Here, boy. Be nice and give us our hat."

The dog obeyed.

Harvey snatched up the hat. They sighed with relief, not wanting to return to their new parents with the announcement of a lost straw hat. As it was, the brim was torn, tattered by the dog's teeth. They examined it, shook their heads.

"Dog, now look what you did. *Schem dich*."

The dog was certainly not ashamed. He bounced around on all fours, whining and begging for attention. The boys touched the top of his head, then boldly ran their hands along his back, where the long black hair parted in the middle, falling down on either side in a luxurious flow, like a girl's hair before her mam wet it and rolled it back.

The dog had small brown eyes, set far apart in his head, a huge, grinning black mouth with a gigantic pink tongue that flapped when he smiled. His skin was loose, his feet were huge. Long hairs grew all along his legs to his feet. There was no collar, no sign of anyone owning this dog.

They put their arms around his neck and squeezed. He slobbered his pink tongue all over their faces. They closed their eyes and laughed.

They rolled in the snow, playing with this soft, kindhearted animal. They chased each other in circles, till they all piled in a big heap, took long breaths, and laughed some more.

Together, they retrieved the sled, rode down the hill, over and over, the dog lolloping by their side, then on the sled with one of them.

When the sun cast a reddish glow on the hillside and the air around them turned pink, they knew they'd overstayed. Shamefaced, their cheeks red with cold, their hats smashed on their heads, hiding their eyebrows, they walked slowly into the forebay, the sled resting by the side of the barn, the dog keeping watch, sitting upright and serious.

The milking had already started, the kerosene lantern casting a yellow glow above the backs of the black-and-white Holsteins, the air heavy with their breath, silage, and warm milk.

Ephraim put away his milking stool, dumped his bucket of frothy milk into the strainer setting on a galvanized milk can, and looked at them. The shamed faces and torn straw hat softened his heart. The dog softened it ever more.

He grinned his slow, easy grin, tickled the dog's head with his large round fingers, and said it looked as if they'd found a faithful buddy, now hadn't they?

# Chapter Three

CHRISTMAS MORNING ARRIVED.

The boys were awakened by the sound of feet dashing past the door of their room, suppressed shrieks, and small tittering sounds.

Henry grabbed Harvey's arm beneath the covers, hissed a dry-throated question, his heart pounding.

"You think the house is on fire?"

Rapid breathing was his only answer.

Four eyes stared wide-eyed at the ceiling. Four hands clutched the quilts as they trembled beneath them. What could have caused the girls to run that way?

They stayed still, their ears strained to hear any sounds that would help them understand what was going on.

More shrieks.

They heard Ephraim and Rachel's voices, although no one seemed especially alarmed. They sniffed. No smoke, so far.

Then they heard their names being called.

"Ya," they answered as one voice.

"Come on down. It's Christmas morning!"

Bewildered, they dressed, tucking wrinkled shirt-tails into freshly washed trousers, snapping suspenders in place as they went downstairs.

They had never experienced Christmas morning. Too poor to buy or make Christmas gifts, the Rueben Esh family did without presents, although they always received a peppermint stick or an orange from Grandfather Beiler. Never both.

Their eyes widened to see the three girls, Malinda, Katie, and Anna sitting on the floor, brown paper wrappings strewn like fluttering birds around them. Their faces were shining, their eyes bright. Between them was a tiny porcelain tea set, white with delicate purple violets etched on the little plates and cups. The teapot had a little spout and a lid you could take off and put back on. This was Katie's Christmas gift.

Anna was holding a rag doll in her arms, her face bent over the doll's white, upturned face. Black eyes and eyelashes were sewn on the face, brown yarn was stitched into the head and braided into two stiff braids on either side. The nose and mouth were embroidered in red.

"Her name is Lucy. Lucy Miriam Wenger," she announced.

The twins nodded solemnly, their dark eyes showing their respect and admiration to Lucy Miriam Wenger. She was a pretty rag doll.

Malinda cradled a pale blue brush and comb set on her lap. There were scrolls of gold all over the back of the brush and across the comb. It was nestled in a silk-lined box that she could open and close with a very small gold latch. For once, she was quiet, even reverent, admiring her gift.

Anna told them these gifts were from the *Grischt Kindly*. During the night, the *Grisht Kindly* brought gifts of kindness to children.

He had brought a gift for the boys too.

Rachel pushed them gently to the sofa, where they sat waiting till she placed a box on their laps. Each box was about as big as a shoebox, wrapped in brown paper packaging.

"Go ahead. Open it."

They had never opened a package, so they weren't sure how. Their fingers scraped across the smooth top, searching for a splice or dent in the paper.

Ephraim smiled.

"Just rip it off," Malinda said, bossy.

So they did.

The box was red, white, and black, with the words *Canadian Flyer* written sideways across it. When they saw the picture of black figure skates, their heads turned toward each other and they both said the exact same thing: "Skates!"

"Did you ever own a pair?" Ephraim asked.

"Oh no. Never. We could just slide on the ice with our boots. But we watched Danny and Bennie, already."

"Now you can learn to skate. Malinda will show you how it's done."

"What do you say, boys?" Rachel asked, not unkindly.

"*Denke. Denke.*"

"You're welcome."

And then because they were so shy, and receiving this kind of gift was almost more than they could comprehend, their faces turned pink, and they blinked rapidly. This kindness made them uncomfortable, as if the family would expect something in return, and they had nothing. Perhaps in the end, they would fail, horribly, at some major task, something that was expected of them that they could not fulfill. But for now, they would accept the skates and try not to let the thought bother them.

Breakfast was pancakes and maple syrup, eggs and fresh *ponhaus*, stewed saltine crackers in hot milk, and grape juice. It was a breakfast fit for a king, Ephraim said, smiling at Rachel, who sipped her tea and waved a hand to banish the flowery words of praise before she was caught with a case of *hochmut*.

Finally, Henry had the nerve to ask if the dog was still here. Ephraim had done the morning chores by himself, only Rachel helping with the milking, as a treat for Christmas Day.

"Yep, he's still here. I put the wooden doghouse in the corner of the forebay, filled it with clean straw for him. He'll have plenty of things to eat with the leftovers Mama gives him, a dish of milk here and there. If I have to, I'll get a bag of Purina dog food from the mill, although that would be an extra expense, of course. We can't let the dog go hungry."

His face turned serious. "Now I hope you realize, boys, that someone could show up and claim the dog. This is not a common breed, so don't get too attached to him."

They shook their heads no, already sidling toward the *kesslehaus*, their faces attentive to what he was saying. They couldn't get their outerwear on fast enough, stomping around the *kesslehaus* floor to pull the rubber boots up over their black leather shoes.

And there he was. The beautiful, magnificent dog with the long, black hairs on his tail that waved back and forth like a flag of welcome, the smiling black face with the funny brown eyes shaped like a triangle.

"There you are, dog!" shouted Henry. Harvey plowed straight into the big dog with his arms wide open, and closed them somewhere around the region of his neck.

"Dog, dog!" he shouted, squeezing his eyes shut as the enormous pink tongue sloshed all over his face.

They chased each other around the forebay, until the horses began to bang their hooves against the sides of their stalls. They stopped, looked at the frightened animals, and took the dog out in the gray, white morning that hid the sun away from them.

They played all morning. They hitched the dog to the wooden sled with a harness made of bits and pieces of leather and rope they found on the wooden floor of the closet where the driving horses' harnesses hung.

Harvey sat on the sled while Henry led the dog by the makeshift bridle. He ran in circles, trying to see what was behind him, dumping Harvey into the low ditch by the barnyard fence, The dog became tangled in the harness, overturning the sled, and both boys lay on their stomachs, laughing so hard they couldn't get their breath.

"Whew-ee!" Harvey said, letting out all that pent-up air. Henry held his sides. He had to, the way they hurt from laughing.

"He needs a name. We can't keep calling him dog," Henry squeaked, wiping his eyes.

"Puppy?"

"Not Puppy. A dog as big as this?"

"Abraham Lee's have a Puppy."

"That little short haired one?"

"Yes."

"Well, that's different."

Harvey thought awhile.

"What about Bear?"

"Naw. Not Bear. He's way too friendly," Henry snorted.

"I know. Lucky! We're lucky he found us!" Harvey shouted.

"Yeah, Lucky!" Henry shouted, agreement clinched.

So Lucky he was, both in name and adoration.


Christmas Day contained so much joy the twins felt as if they might burst with all of it. For one thing, there were all the cookies, set on the tabletop all day, free, if you wanted one, anytime of the day, even after lunch and before supper.

There was homemade potato candy, made with mashed potatoes and peanut butter, soft little whorls of it spread on the white dough and rolled up like a cinnamon roll. There was some chocolate candy, but only a small amount in a petite glass dish. No more than two, Rachel said. She had to save the rest for tomorrow, which was second Christmas, another day set aside for celebrating that was not as holy as the real Christmas Day. That was when the large amount of aunts and uncles and grandparents and children would arrive.

Henry told Harvey he was not looking forward to it.

Then, after all that ham for supper, they were allowed to pop popcorn on the wood range, and roast chestnuts in the oven.

Malinda said every raw chestnut had a white worm in it, but after it was roasted, the worm turned to powder and became part of the chestnut. You could never eat a raw chestnut or you'd get the worms and die.

Harvey's eyes became big and round. He looked at the tray of roasted chestnuts and rolled one eye toward Henry.

"I am not going to eat them," he whispered.

"They're roasted," Henry answered.

Ephraim cracked so many chestnuts in his mouth, chewed so loud, that Harvey decided the only safe way to spend the evening was to stick with salted popcorn.

Rachel read the story of Jesus' birth from the Bible. The boys had heard it before, of course, with their sad-eyed father gathering his many children about him on Christmas Day and introducing their fledgling souls to the milk of Christianity, which was the Christ Child's birth.

Rachel was a good storyteller.

She said the Baby Jesus was a good baby to be born in the stable with the cows and donkeys and sheep, and He lay quietly in His manger bed filled with straw.

Henry had never thought of that. He elbowed Harvey's ribs and asked what born meant. Harvey didn't know, so he shook his head, told him to be quiet.

They drank cold cider. Ephraim heated his in a saucepan and drank it like coffee.

It was warm and bright in the farmhouse, as the twins sat listening to Rachel's voice rising and falling. They imagined the shepherds in the field, the host of heavenly angels singing to them of Jesus' birth. But as the hour became late, their eyes grew heavy, and they thought only of the dog, Lucky.

The wonderful Christmas Day came to a close when they trudged wearily up the stairs, shed their clothes, and climbed beneath the covers with soft sighs of happiness and contentment. They fell asleep without remembering to say their "*Müde Binnich.*"

Second Christmas arrived a bit differently, having to get out of bed in their frigid, upstairs bedroom, shivering into pants and shirts, then straight to the *kesslehaus* to don their outerwear.

They lifted their faces to the snow that fell sideways, blown in by a steady moaning wind that whipped the bare, black branches in the moonless early morning. They pressed their tattered straw hats on their heads and raced for the warm, steamy barn, closing the cast iron latch firmly behind them.

You'd think Malinda would be friendly, having received that gift on Christmas Day, but she glared at the boys from her crouch on the wooden milking stool, telling them to walk quietly, or they'd scare the cow she was milking, and she'd turn over the bucket of milk if she kicked.

So they said nothing, just went quietly to greet Lucky in the forebay, who wiggled and bounded and jumped all over them, so glad to see his beloved little friends.

They fed the heifers and the horses, by the dim flickering light of the kerosene lantern. Harvey carefully placed two long, yellow ears of corn in the small section of the wooden trough that was worn smooth by the heavy leather halter and the chain attached to each horse. Henry dumped their portion of smooth, slippery oat kernels, and they stood side by side, watching the massive noses in the trough, crunching and chewing.

A horse had an expert way of eating the hard, yellow kernels of corn off a cob. They never ate the cob, just stripped the corn off with their long, yellow teeth and chewed with a steady, popping sound. Some corn fell out of the sides of their mouth, but they lipped it up after the cob was bare.

It was their job to gather up the cobs after the horses were finished and carry them to the tool shed. Ephraim stuck them upright into a bucket that contained a few inches of kerosene, which the cobs would soak up like a sponge. That was what Rachel used to start a fire in the cookstove every morning.

Nothing went to waste on the farm in those days. The twins knew to sweep up every bit of hay to make sure the horses ate all of it. If they spilled oats out of the scoop, they were expected to sweep it up and give it to the horses. Every bit of manure was loaded on the spreader with pitchforks, drawn to the fields with sturdy Belgians, and spread on the land for fertilizer. The gardens and flower beds were also covered with a heavy layer in the fall, where it would decompose, enriching the fertile soil in spring.

Breakfast was oatmeal and toast with apple butter, eaten quickly and quietly. Ephraim knelt by his chair and everyone else followed suit, kneeling by their own bench or chair, as he said the German morning prayer from the *Gebet Buch*. This morning, even his words were spoken faster than usual, with respect to his wife's red face and snapping eyes.

This was the day of the *Grishtdag Essa*.

Dishes were done in double-quick time, the kitchen swept and dusted. Rachel put warm soapy water in a tin basin and proceeded to pull each child's head against her round stomach and scrub. She used no mercy and wasted no time.

The rough washcloth was raked across their faces and around their ears and neck, over and over, her breath above them coming thick and fast.

She felt soft, though, and she smelled of oatmeal and Lava soap. She parted their hair down the middle, removed the snarls with the sturdy comb, patted their heads, and told them to run upstairs and dress in their Sunday clothes.

Harvey stood in the middle of his cold bedroom and explored his ears, from the top to the bottom of his earlobes.

"Guess they're still there."

Henry was pulling on the sleeve of his blue Sunday shirt, trying to slide it off the wire hanger.

"What?"

"My ears."

Henry laughed. The shirt slid off the hanger so he dressed quickly, jumping into the stiff black Sunday trousers. Harvey did the same, then pulled on his black socks.

They stood back and surveyed each other, seriously inspecting their appearance. To be thrust into a world of strangers was a daunting prospect, so they buttoned all their buttons, straightened their collars, and adjusted shirttails and suspenders.

"Should we wear our *chackets*?"

"She didn't say."

They pondered this question.

"Go ask," Henry offered.

At that moment, the doorknob turned and Malinda stuck her head in the door.

"Mam said to wear your *chackets*."

So they did, without answering Malinda.

Now what if they would not have put on their trousers and she stuck her head in like that? Well, they both decided firmly, if that was how she was going to be, then she'd just have to see their thin, white legs and maybe their underpants.

Downstairs, they were told to *raum up* the *kesslehaus*, put away the boots, and sweep any hay or straw that might have been dragged in from the barn.

They obeyed, finished their work, then sat side by side on the sofa, unsure what was expected of them from here on out. When they felt like this, it was always comforting to feel the touch of the other twin's shoulder, each boy knowing he was not alone. That was when Malinda came blustering in from the *kesslhaus* saying the boys had not shaken the rugs.

Rachel was mixing celery into the bread cubes for the *roasht*. She never missed a beat, just flung words over her shoulder, telling Malinda she didn't ask them to do that. If she thought it necessary, she could go ahead and do it.

Katie and Anna were freshly watered down and combed so tightly, they had a surprised look with those lifted eyebrows. On either side of their foreheads, their dark hair was rolled in, stretched into two long rolls and wound around a steel hairpin in the back, forming thick coils of rolled hair with the hairpin centered exactly in the middle, on the outside, with about a dozen more stuck into the rolled coils to keep the hair in place.

The boys thought it must be an awful thing, being a girl and having to go through all that. They remembered their own sisters and missed them, especially Emma and Annie, who were older than both of them.

Henry swallowed, as his eyes turned soft and liquid, wondering if they thought about their brothers often, or if they were already forgotten.

They tried to be brave, but their hearts quaked when the gray buggies began to arrive, filling the house with all kinds of strangers the boys had never seen. At times like this, they wanted to go home, even if it was a sad, poverty-infused home, it was still the home they knew.

So many people, so many voices.

Black shawls and bonnets, children wearing *mondlin*, those lined wraps with shoulder capes that buttoned down the front, a matching bonnet in purple or blue. Babies unwrapped like Christmas gifts, sisters and cousins pawing at scarves and tiny black shawls, peering into brand-new faces to exclaim over the hair or the likeness to Uncle Rufus or Aunt Hettie.

Perhaps Cousin Barbara.

Henry and Harvey remained on the sofa, wishing they could turn into pillows.

No one took notice of them, so they stayed quiet, their dark eyes not quite focused on everyone and no one.

Finally from the din, there emerged an old, old woman dressed in black all over. She was short, bent forward at the waist, round like an egg, with her gnarled old hands spread over her cane like tree roots. From beneath the hem of her skirt, two black shoes shuffled over and stopped in front of the boys.

"*Vell. Voss hen ma do?*"

One of her scary looking hands was extended toward them, so Harvey obeyed his training and put his hand into it.

As scaly as a dry fish. But he shook hands.

"*Schoene boova. Ztzvilling.*"

They looked up into a face so riven and crisscrossed with cracks and wrinkles that it barely resembled a face. There were hairy warts or moles all over the place. One on the end of her nose. Her eyes were almost closed off by flaps of skin, and she had no teeth.

"How old are you, boys?"

"We are seven," Harvey whispered.

"What? Speak up! I don't hear well."

"We are seven."

"Oh. *Sivva*. Do you go to school?"

Rachel disengaged herself from a conversation with a sister-in-law and came to the boys' rescue.

"Boys, this is a great-grandmother. *An gros grus-mommy*. She is 97. Her name is Fronie Stoltzfus."

The boys didn't say anything to that, but thought she must have been in the Garden of Eden somewhere. Ninety-seven years old was so old you could hardly think on it.

They breathed easier when Rachel led her away, relieved to stop being accountable for being only seven and not belonging to this family in the true sense of the word.

Although a constant stream of children paraded past the sofa, no one stopped or offered to play with them. Little eyes watched from behind chair backs, even smaller ones stood in front of them and glared, a thumb stuck into a pink mouth, saliva dripping on aprons or shirtfronts.

They waited a long time to be seated for Christmas dinner. All the men and boys ate at the first table, a table that extended the whole way across the kitchen and into the living room.

Wonderful smells came from the platters of steaming *roasht*, the white mounds of mashed potatoes with browned butter running down the sides, and puddling along the rim of the serving dish. There were cooked green beans, stewed turnips, and sweet potatoes. Celery cooked in a vinegary white sauce, applesauce, shredded cabbage and carrots, pickled red beets, and sweet pickles. Chow-chow and cooked peas. Homemade egg noodles.

The twins sat on the sofa, watched the dishes being passed from one hand to the next. They watched burly red-faced men lifting mountainous spoonfuls of everything, causing them some anxiety.

Would there be anything left?

Mince meat pie, pumpkin pie, and apple pie. Chocolate cake and grape mush. Vanilla cornstarch pudding and strawberry dessert. White cake and spice cake.

Still the men kept eating, talking, and laughing. When they finally folded their hands in their laps and bent their heads to thank God for their full stomachs, Henry sighed with satisfaction.

The dishes were cleared, washed and dried, set back on the table, and all the women and girls were seated.

Rachel and another woman the twins did not know stayed by the stove to serve the table. No one took notice of Henry and Harvey. Again, the dishes were passed, the women ate and ate, served the girls, talked and laughed, and enjoyed themselves immensely.

A lone tear appeared on Henry's eyelash, fell, leaving a wet streak on his cheek. He was hungry, afraid everyone had forgotten them, and did not know how to go about making his presence known without seeming bold. Harvey glanced over, then slid closer, pressing his shoulder against Henry's.

"We'll eat with our Rachel," he whispered.

Henry nodded, his brown eyes met those of his twin, comfort passed and accepted.

And they did.

The table was set for a third time, although only to about half its length. There was plenty of food to go around. Women hovered over them with serving dishes, platters of steaming *roasht*, and bowls of potatoes. The boys lifted their spoons and ate and ate till they could hold no more. Then they tasted the chocolate cake with the cornstarch pudding, and after that, the pumpkin pie.

Rachel smiled so sweetly at them, as she kept pushing more pie in their direction. She asked softly if they had made new friends. They shook their heads, ashamed now.

"It's all right. You will after dinner," she said.

She introduced Cousin Bennie from Kirkwood. He was tall and blond, blue eyed and fair skinned. His hair was cut high on his forehead, but along the length of his ears, it wasn't cut, so that only the tips of his upper ears pushed through the straight yellow hair.

"Hi!" he said loudly.

"Hi!" answered Harvey, then Henry.

"Twins?" he asked.

They both nodded at once.

"I'm Bennie Beiler. My dad is your dad's brother. Aquilla. Well, they say Ephraim isn't your real dad, but you're here now, so we're cousins."

The twins smiled shyly, checking Bennie's face for signs of disapproval. He seemed genuine.

Together, they sat on the *kesslehaus* floor and tugged on their rubber boots. Five more boys came to join them, all aged between six and twelve. Bennie introduced them by age: Homer, Eli, Dannie, Amos, and Gideon. The boys acknowledged each one.

They brought Lucky out from his doghouse and the fun began. Snow swirled around them as they hitched the excited dog to the wooden sled. They raced and rolled and tumbled, the big, loose-jointed dog galloping along full speed, dragging the sled filled with cheering boys, his tongue dangling like a long pink ribbon.

Malinda appeared with a gaggle of scarved girls, who wanted to use the sled to go sledding on the hill. They stood there like different sizes of fence posts with their hands hanging uselessly, waiting and glaring till the boys gave up and unhitched Lucky. They stood there so long, snow accumulated on the tops of their heads and their shoulders, like big grains of sugar. Malinda told the boys to put that dog in the doghouse, he was tired out. Didn't they have any sense?

Bennie eyed her with full-out dislike, reached down and scooped up a handful of snow, packed it in two cupped hands, and let it fly.

Smack!

Bennie knew he was in for it the minute that snowball hit her bossy face. Malinda yelled, scooped up a handful of snow, her eyes streaming with melting snow, unable to focus properly, the snowball yards from her intended target.

That whole afternoon the twins had more fun than they ever had before. They flung snowballs from a fort, ducked and yelled and rolled over and washed each other's faces with handfuls of snow.

Malinda called a truce and gave everyone the same chance to build a proper fort. Henry and Harvey rolled snowballs, wrapped their arms around them to lift them high, packed them together, and smoothed them over. The fort was v-shaped and built for strength.

Snowballs whizzed by, knocking straw and black felt hats off the boys' heads, splattering all over the girls' scarves, splatting into walls and the snow-covered ground in front.

Barn cats scuttled along walls, casting apprehensive glances at the war in the driveway. Lucky whined in his doghouse, but Malinda made him stay there. Bennie asked if she was always the boss, and she said no, but the twins nodded their heads behind her back, creating a look of glee on Bennie's face.

Then they were called in to sing German Christmas songs. Slumped shoulders and quiet groans of protest were followed by disgusted expressions and snowballs flung away without aim.

Singing hymns at *S' Grishtag Essa* was nothing short of a punishment. The house was overheated, the men sat in strict and holy circles of righteousness, while the women spread their skirts across their knees, pursed their lips, and hung their eyebrows at a humble angle, trying to erase the fact that they had gossiped about Amos Fisher's Lena, who turned sixteen in January and would bring her parents to shame.

The children all had to sit still, hold the fat hymnbook as if they could read or understand one word of German. It wasn't so bad when they sang the fast tunes of "*Schtille Nacht, Heilige Nacht*" or "*Freue Dich, Velt,*" but when the men began the slow, laborious plainsong, bellowing out the words of old hymns from the Ausbund, they knew the snowball fight was in the past.

Rachel served grape juice and cider after the children thought they surely wouldn't start another song, only to hear the trembling vocals of yet another uncle. Bowls of popcorn seasoned with salt, then gold popcorn balls, sticky and crunchy with brown sugar and molasses, followed the juice and cider. Once the singers wet their throats with grape juice, they began wailing on, although the children soon recognized their gateway to freedom lay in the heavy platter of popcorn balls. Sure enough, the minute they began to eat, the singing stopped, and they were free to go.

The headlong dash to the *kesslehaus* was halted by anxious mothers who were thinking of the ride home and all that wet outerwear. They helped the children dry their clothes on wooden racks, brought out the checkers and Parcheesi games, served more cookies and warm cups of spearmint tea.

Henry and Harvey draped themselves over the backs of kitchen chairs and watched Bennie beat Malinda at checkers. Bennie was smart. Smarter than anyone they had ever met. He could build the best fort, and move the checkers to just the right spot. Plus, he had a pony, he said. Anyone who owned a pony was smart and rich and luckier than anyone they had ever known.

The Christmas dinner wound down when Ephraim began to watch the clock, stretch his arms above his head, and make strange, exaggerated yawns.

"Chore time," he said.

Reluctantly, the brothers and sisters gathered up their various offspring, braved the cold and oncoming twilight, amid heartfelt thanks and much handshaking, words of goodbye and well wishes.

*S' Grishtag Essa* was over for another year.

The house was in complete disarray, but with Rachel barking orders, the girls sweeping the floors and washing the dishes, and the twins sent to the barn to help do the chores, life returned to normal before they went to bed.

The best part of winter was yet to come, when they would watch the farm pond freeze over and be able to try out the most wonderful gifts in the whole world: those Canadian Flyers.

# Chapter Four

AFTER SECOND CHRISTMAS DAY, THE TWINS finally went to school, carrying their books in a paper bag, a black metal lunchbox containing a slice of buttered bread, a jar of milk, and a sugar cookie.

Their new home was not far from the one where they had spent their first six years, so they went to the same school as their birth brothers and sisters. They were hesitant and shy at first, but before the week was up, they accepted everything as the new normal on both sides.

Mrs. Dayble had not repented of her ill temper, so things remained the same as far as scrunching down in your seat, hoping it wasn't something you had done that made her walk like that. So hopping mad, she rocked from side to side, before twisting misbehaving Emanuel Lantze's shirtsleeve, which was sure to contain the skin of his arm. Sure enough, he clapped his left hand over his right forearm, lowered his shoulders, opened his mouth in a silent howl of protest, then squeezed shut as he absorbed the pain.

Harvey shivered in his shoes watching Emanuel. He bent his head and resumed his studies, muttering "two times six is twelve, two times seven is fourteen," and so forth.

Henry's eyes snapped his disapproval of so harsh a punishment for merely tweaking Helen's pigtails. Emanuel wouldn't do that if she would quit turning around, pointing at his mistakes. She'd told him once that his handwriting was worse than chicken scratch, so she had it coming.

The redbrick school was nestled in a group of maple trees with a slope of pasture rising on each side. The front porch was on the gable end, where the roof came to a V, and there were three windows on either side, with two on the porch. There was a huge cast iron furnace toward the front of the room that often burned red-hot, heating the front half of the classroom but not the back. There was a row of blackboards along the front, a wooden tray along the bottom that contained chalk and erasers. The floor was wooden, wide, thick oak boards that were oiled in the fall before school started. The desks were wooden, varnished to a glossy sheen, with cast iron legs and a hinged seat you could put up or down. The seat was attached to the front of the desk behind, so there was a long row of desks and seats down throughout the room.

Five rows of eight desks, all filled with children.

One teacher.

Her desk was up front by the blackboard, and she stood behind it mostly, like a bald eagle with big yellow eyes with no eyelids, and a powerful hooked beak.

Henry figured she could probably kill a fish with her nose. Of course, he never said that to anyone, not even Harvey. He just thought it.

Mrs. Dayble's classroom was quiet. The children learned their lessons. If they didn't behave, she administered her famous pinch, and if that didn't thwart the problem, the ruler did. If any parent complained about her methods of discipline, she lifted her chin, crossed her arms, and told them to come teach the school if they could do better. No one ever did, and she had taught school in Leacock Township for thirty-two years.

Lucky stayed on. Sometimes when an automobile or a horse and buggy came rolling into the Ephraim

King farm, the boys would peer fearfully out of the barn door, or peek out a window in the house, wondering yet again if it would be Lucky's owner, coming to take their pet.

But it never was.

They had many happy Christmas days at their new home. They grew to think of Ephraim and Rachel as Dat and Mam, while their biological parents faded into a murky background of memories of their very young childhood. They remembered the good times and the transition between families with a twinge, although nothing that would hamper their ability to grow and learn, to become decent, obedient boys who learned to love and respect their new parents. They always understood the Esh family's poverty, being unable to feed the growing number of children, and understood too that Ephraim King needed boys, and they filled that need, which always served to satisfy the questioning inside. That, and the love Ephraim and Rachel had for the boys, constantly showing their caring in many ways.

Lucky was a constant companion. Everywhere the boys went, there was Lucky, the huge black dog lolloping by their side. In the cold of winter, in snow and ice, in the heat of summer, through the scattered leaves of autumn, there was Lucky. It was a rare and special bond, one the Amish folks talked about for years to come.

Five Christmases came and went, creating more happy memories for them as they grew. They were twelve years old that spring of 1941. Lancaster County was pummeled with snowstorm after snowstorm that winter. Belgian horses and trustworthy mules plowed through six-foot drifts, hauling cans of milk to the creamery. For days at a time, no trucks or automobiles could navigate the roads. Men with snow shovels, graders, makeshift snow pushers, and draggers were everywhere.

And then it began to rain in late March, swelling the rivers and creeks to a dangerous brown surge filled with chunks of ice as big as a shed. Patches of slush moved along like lace cloth, bits of wood and dead tree branches roiled and bumped, staying against the trunks of trees, before the current pulled them away, hurling them along.

The Susquehanna River overflowed its banks, the dead water crept past its banks across the road and into the stately homes built along its banks in the city of Harrisburg.

There was nothing to be done but call the situation an emergency and evacuate. Everywhere there were misplaced folks, living with relatives, in empty buildings, or they left the county entirely. The people of Lancaster County had woes of their own. Cows became stranded in pastures on high ground, unable to navigate the many swollen creeks that sluiced their way in brown, foaming currents that looked like dirty dishwater.

Gray clouds hung over the land, repeatedly releasing yet another rain shower, deepening and widening the already overflowing creeks.

Ephraim offered to take the boys to school that morning, saying it didn't look as if the rain had any notion of letting up. Harvey said, nah, they'd walk. "It's not raining now."

So they grabbed their black, tin lunch pails, donned their collarless black coats and straw hats, and were stopped on their way out the door with admonishment to wait on Katie and Anna.

So they did, shifting their weight from foot to foot, watching the door without patience. A robin chirped constantly in the crabapple tree by the *kesslehaus*, so they deserted their post and went to see what all the commotion was about.

Of course, before they found the nest she was building, the girls appeared in their royal-blue bonnets and black shawls, telling them to get down from there, it was time to go.

They had a two-mile walk, which they didn't consider being too far or too strenuous. It was actually a very nice walk on most days, even in winter, with ice to slide on, snowballs to make, walking with Ben Stoltzfus' children after the first mile. So much to talk about with Willie and Rueben. Much the same as all the other farm boys, there were endless discussions about the animals, the pastures and woods, conjuring up half-truths to impress one another, as children will.

This morning, they were not at the end of the back lane that led to their farm, so they walked on.

When a horse and buggy pulled up beside them, Ben's friendly face beamed down at them.

"*Vedta mitt?*"

The girls willingly clambered aboard, but Henry and Harvey looked at each other and shook their heads, both thinking there might still be time to hurl a few branches into the swollen Pequea Creek, by the side of the red covered bridge.

"All right then!" Ben called, pulled on the reins, and chirped to his horse. The buggy rumbled away, spitting gravel beneath the steel wagon wheel rims.

Immediately, the boys took off. They ran gleefully, their mouths wide, their lunches swinging, knocking against their legs. When the covered bridge was in sight, they increased their speed, their breath coming in hard little puffs, their cheeks red with the damp air.

Over the stone wall, down the slippery grassy slope beneath.

"Whoa!" Henry shouted.

"Whoa!" Harvey echoed.

The brown water was right there. Right at their feet. The Pequea Creek spread out like an ocean before them. They stood side by side, their shoulders touching, mesmerized, watching the powerful surge from beneath the bridge. Only a few yards from the base of the bridge and rising. That was when they spotted the little brown dog. Whimpering and crying, thin and shivering, he was stuck on a stone ledge, a small shelf of stone so narrow he could barely stay on, inches above the water. When he saw the boys, he cried like a real baby, begging and yelping.

"Aw!" Henry whispered.

"If we had a stick. . ." Harvey muttered.

"He couldn't hang on to a stick."

"Maybe."

All thoughts of school and tardiness vanished. They were single-minded in their purpose. The dog must be rescued.

They turned, searched the weeds and trees by the side of the road. They picked up and discarded a few puny branches, but nothing that was long enough to reach the poor, frightened animal. They turned as one, both noticed the loose board on the bridge. All it would take was a hefty yank to loosen it.

"Damage to the bridge," Henry said, seriously.

"What else can we do?" Harvey asked.

"Would it be long enough?"

"I believe so."

They scrambled up over the stone wall. Both grabbed the red board and pulled upward, then pushed. The rusty nails groaned. They worked at loosening it, pushing, then yanking sideways, till the board loosened, slid sideways, and fell with a *whump*.

Immediately they picked it up, ran to the stone wall, and shoved it over. The little brown dog's eyes were large and brown and pleading. His cries increased.

The deep brown water roiled out from under the bridge, carrying logs and branches, a dead cat with slimy fur matted to its body, boards, and clumps of brown weeds and brambles.

Side by side, the twins hung over the stone wall above the water, straining to angle the board just to the dog, near enough to be able to guide him up over his dangerous perch.

Only a foot.

"I'll lean over, you hang on to my waist," Harvey instructed.

"Don't, Harvey. What if you slip?" Henry warned.

"I'll be careful."

Henry felt Harvey's shoulder leave his. He slid his arm around his waist as he leaned over, straining to acquire a few more inches to reach the whining, stranded animal. He got the board situated on the ledge. The dog lowered its head, ready to step out, when the board slipped on the slick, wet stones, went down with a splash, taking the dog with it.

It overbalanced Harvey.

The weight was too much for Henry.

It happened in the blink of an eye. Harvey tore out of Henry's grasp, leaving him with a hoarse, choking scream and empty arms.

He could only watch Harvey hit the brown water, the red board and the little dog going before him, submerged in the dangerous current that was suddenly wicked, evil. The deep, powerful sound of rushing water meant death and destruction.

Henry left the stone wall and slid in the wet grass. He waved his arms and screamed. He cried. He begged Harvey to swim, swim, Harvey. He saw Harvey's straw hat round the bend.

Harvey's head appeared above the water, his face white, his brown eyes terrified. He thrashed his arms to stay afloat, then disappeared around the bend with the board and the dog.

Henry called and called.

He could not race along the bank to follow Harvey's progress. The briars and undergrowth grew too thick and heavy. The thought that Harvey would make it seized him. He was a good swimmer in the farm pond. Every summer he became a better one. Ben Stoltzfus' Willie said he was like a fish.

Henry climbed over the stone wall, his breath coming in hot puffs of terror. He cried, moaned, muttered to himself. He found he was uttering the word "please, please" over and over, begging for help from a much Higher Power from his soul, without knowing he was capable of such deep immortal pleading.

There were no automobiles or teams, horses and buggies, nothing, that morning.

So Henry ran. He ran to the schoolhouse, often stumbling and falling, till his trousers were torn and blood seeped from his torn kneecap. He burst through the front door, an ashen-faced, terrified specter that stayed in tender children's minds, rendering them unable to sleep, concerned mothers sitting with them as they lay wide-eyed, asking questions about death and God and the reason why He let Harvey Esh slide into that awful brown water.

Mrs. Dayble turned, disapproval for her tardy scholars pulled firmly in place. It melted away at the sight before her.

Quickly, she laid down her hymn book, walked to his side to place a now shaking hand on his shoulder.

"He fell in, he fell in," he said, hoarsely, between panting breaths.

"Who? What are you talking about?" Mrs. Dayble asked, her own breath coming in hard puffs.

"H. . . H. . . Harvey."

The class had stopped singing at Henry's appearance.

Thirty-eight pupils, lined up by size, in five rows, stood silently, in shocked disbelief, straining to hear what their classmate was trying to convey. Faces turned pale, eyes grew large and dark.

Mrs. Dayble grasped Henry's shoulder. "Tell me what happened."

Between coughs and panting breaths, the story came out, wrung from Henry's mind by necessity.

Mrs. Dayble straightened, strode purposefully to the coat rack, got down her old beige woolen coat, barked strict orders for everyone to return to their seats and stay there, she was going to use the telephone.

When she let herself out the door, Henry went to his own seat, sagged wearily into it, and began to sob, quietly, restrainedly.

Katie went to him, slid in his seat beside him, an arm stealing about his heaving shoulders. Anna began to cry in earnest, her friend Salome hurrying to sit with her, the childish intuition of providing instant comfort.

The classroom was silent, save for the sounds of quiet weeping. No one asked questions. No one tried to get Henry to talk. They were still absorbing bits and pieces of Henry's words to Mrs. Dayble.

When she returned, the fire sirens had already started, the high, thin wail reaching out an arm and pulling them without mercy into a stark and awful reality. Something had happened. Something terrible.

Henry stayed in his seat, with Katie's support. Mrs. Daybel asked the children to fold their hands on top of their desks and pray that Harvey would be safe.

They came for Henry.

Concerned parents and neighbors showed up, gathered up their children, thanking God for their safety.

Henry stood by the stone wall talking to the men from the firehouse. He told them precisely, in calm, measured tones what had occurred. It was only when Ephraim and Rachel appeared that he lost all resolve and cried deep, groaning sobs of despair.

His sad-eyed father and overwhelmed mother appeared later, when it began to rain. They stood by Henry, said Harvey's time was up, God had chosen to take him. Henry peered up into their faces, squinted his eyes, and said nothing. Ephraim said they would search along the Pequea, perhaps they'd find him alive. He was a good swimmer.

All his older brothers and sisters arrived in buggies, tied their horses to a telephone pole, came to stand with Henry, staring at him as if he had a strange disease they did not want to contract.

No one spoke to him, so he turned his back and looked out over the Pequea Creek that had grasped his brother in its dirty, brown arms and sucked the life out of him. He hated the creek. The feeling dried up his tears of agony and clenched his fists into tense, white-knuckled misery.

When the rain increased, the group of watchers moved under the shelter of the bridge to wait for any word of Harvey's rescue. Ephraim and Rueben left to help with the search.

All day, each side of the Pequea swarmed with firemen, police, neighbors and well-wishers, members of the Amish, Mennonite, Dunkard, Lutheran, and Catholic communities, all united as one to find Harvey.

When night fell, they took Henry home.

Groups of women inhabited the kitchen of Ephraim King, making coffee, serving sandwiches and cookies, as if in sheer amounts they could somehow lighten the shock and pain of this awful happening.

Malinda had not seen Henry, having opted to stay at home till her parents returned. She was the kind of person who dealt with stress of any kind with action. Alone, she milked all the cows, fed the calves, heifers, and horses without getting tired or slowing down, propelled by a nervous, almost manic energy.

Now, she stood in front of her distressed, broken-down brother and said bluntly, "Don't ever blame yourself, Henry. You'll suffer later on if you do."

It was a strange, hard way of greeting, but for some reason or other, those words often rose up like the wings of a powerful bird, to lift him above the wondering and the regret of what had happened that rainy morning on their way to school.

No one slept.

Henry dozed fitfully on the couch, to awaken a few minutes later with the ghost of Harvey sliding out of his grasp like a knife to his senses.

Oh, Harvey. Harvey. How will I ever go through the future without you? It was like reaching the edge of a cliff to look out over an arid, dead landscape filled with gray, jutting rocks and no water. He could see no way of survival.

Hope that Harvey would still be alive afforded a bit of comfort. It was only when reality set in, a grim-faced policeman's arrival to announce the finding of Harvey's drowned form, caught in a pile of debris at the dam, that Henry tore out of Rachel's grasp, sobbing in silent heaves, ran to the barn, pushing aside bystanders and other folks who wished to convey comfort, to find Lucky.

Lucky, the Christmas dog, still the best companion. He threw himself down, buried his face in Lucky's thick, black hair, and sobbed out the despair and pain and loss, taking in the comfort of the faithful friend's warmth and the stirring of love that ensured his lone survival.

If Lucky was here, he was not alone.

Grown men wept.

When they brought the body of his brother back from the funeral home, Davis and Wendell, in the city of Lancaster, Lucky stood by Henry's side, his small triangular brown eyes fixed on Harvey's still, pale face.

The house was prepared for the viewing. Two neighboring couples were appointed to take charge of the proceedings, as was the Amish custom. The house was filled with friends and relatives dressed in black, sober-faced women and somber men, weeping classmates and cousins.

Two sets of parents, both feeling the loss keenly.

It was Mattie's way to remain stoic, stone-faced, and silent.

Neighbors questioned this, in huddled groups of whispers, eyes cast accusingly, doubts put forth into the room like an obscuring fog.

Doesn't she care? Has the woman no feelings for her twins?

The truth was hidden away, beneath the pinned black cape that hung well below her shoulders. She cared. Had cared too much, the day the twins were taken away. No one except her husband and children knew of her breakdown, hidden away in the *Komma* as she struggled to maintain her grasping hope of keeping her sanity when the waters of her agony threatened to pull her under. She had died, in a way, like Harvey, locked away in a darkened room, the green blinds drawn behind the white cotton curtains that reached only halfway up the window frame.

Though the children of Reuben's first wife, she had loved each boy, gazing into their perfect, cherubic faces and loving them with her soft mother heart. She had fiercely resisted this giving away of the twins, but, in the end, submitted to the will of her struggling, over-worked, sad-eyed husband, unable to make ends meet.

For she loved Rueben as well.

Yes, she cared.

But she had reached a peaceful plain where caring, like her will, was diminished and taken away, re-placed by survival, looking forward to the day when her Lord and Savior returned with all His angels to take her home to Heaven, where there was no fear of poverty, only indescribable happiness and singing in gold mansions that He had prepared for her.

The sun burst through the scudding gray clouds on the day of Harvey's burial, casting a bright, golden glow over the graveyard close to Gordonville. The huddled group of mourners dressed in black lifted to-ward Heaven in spirit as the gray-haired bishop read the closing prayer.

For years, folks talked about the big black dog that stood at the gravesite, Henry's hand resting on his head. The kindhearted bishop had made allowance, seeing how the black dog was the only comfort for the remaining twin.

When the men shoveled the wet clods of dirt onto the lowered casket, it was Henry and Lucky that stood foremost, watching attentively, the dog peering down into the grave with his sad, triangular brown eyes. He whimpered once. Henry reached down to stroke his head, quieting him.

Buds broke forth from sodden, wet branches that day. Robins and sparrows chirped and flitted about, getting down to the business of nest-building, filling the air with their ambitious songs. Horses plodded in pastures, black-and-white Holsteins tore at clumps of new grass, and baby lambs frolicked on ungainly legs between the watchful eyes of their mothers.

Life went on.

For Mattie, it was another beginning, her pain hidden away as the breakdown had been, swept away and never talked about, never brought into the general public, as was the custom.

Rueben took care of his quiet wife to the best of his ability, all their children gathered around their table.

But in Mattie's heart, there remained a special place for her Henry and his black dog.

# Chapter Five

GROWING UP, HENRY OFTEN FELT AS IF THERE was only half of him remaining. He became used to looking up from his chores, to show Harvey the biggest night crawler he ever saw, or to tell him about the bass in the pool by the sycamore tree.

The space in his heart occupied by Harvey was left empty, scraped and raw, so that sometimes, he would clutch his shirtfront, pulling the fabric and row of sturdy buttons away from his skin, to ease the pain, to be able to breathe.

It was those times that turned him to Lucky. They would roam the fields and woods together, especially that first summer without Harvey. There was no greater comfort than being alone with the huge, black dog, settling together on the bank of the Pequea Creek, sitting side by side the way he sat with Harvey.

Lucky was trained well. He knew instinctively when Henry was watching for any movement in the deep, amber pool, where the water eddied by the sycamore tree. If they sat quietly, from time to time, the flash of a fat bass or catfish would catch Henry's eye.

Lucky's ears pointed up then, but no one but Henry knew this, the way they were mostly buried in the thick hair that grew all over him. Lucky was the most intelligent dog.

Even when the fish swam into view, he did not bounce up and down or whine. He stayed right where he was supposed to, waiting politely for a spoken command from his master.

Ephraim and Rachel believed Henry should open up about his loss, at least talk about Harvey at times when they could tell he was suffering. But he never did.

It was Malinda who caught Henry talking to Lucky, telling him all about the day at the bridge.

One evening about three months after Harvey's death, she came to her mother on a hot, humid evening, when the sun still felt too uncomfortably warm, even at that hour. The heat still clung to the sides of the house and turned the grass warm and limp.

Rachel sat on the creaking old porch swing, its rusted iron chains attached to the thick metal hooks from the beam in the ceiling, screeching melodiously. Her hands were never idle, so tonight she was shelling a few leftover peas she found still clinging to the decaying vines.

Malinda strode up to the porch in her purposeful manner, eyed her mother, and stood before her with her hands on her hips.

"Mam, Henry talks to Lucky. I heard him. You had better have him checked by a doctor. I'm pretty sure there is something wrong with his brain."

Rachel looked at her daughter, unruffled, acquainted with her theatrics.

"I'm serious. You should have heard him. He had a long story, over and over, about the dog stuck on the stone ledge, the board. He said the water was like a brown dragon that licked up Harvey. He shouldn't be talking like that."

Rachel considered her words, then told Malinda perhaps it was a good thing if he talked to his dog, if he couldn't bring himself to talk to anyone else.

"But it isn't normal," Malinda insisted.

"Perhaps for Henry it is," Rachel said. "You must consider, he is working through a terrible loss, one you and I can't understand. He doesn't feel close to any of us, with good reason, so we need to respect his privacy. Leave him alone when you hear him talking to Lucky."

Malinda cast a sidelong look at her mother before letting herself in through the screen door.

So the summer heat intensified as July came to a close. The large vegetable patch took up most of Rachel and the girls' time, pulling weeds and hoeing, harvesting, and mulching. The tomatoes were hanging in thick green clusters, some of them with hints of orange on their round cheeks. Cucumber vines were thick and heavy with large, medium-size, and small ones hiding beneath the prickly leaves. The yellow ears of corn turned full and sweet, so Henry was told to help Mam and the girls all day. He found himself in the early light of morning, sticky with corn silk and showers of dew from the wide, abrasive corn leaves that slapped against his face and shoulders.

The sun was like a giant orange ball of pulsing heat, already so early in the morning, so Henry pushed through the stalks of corn, ripping off each golden ear with a swift, downward move, held them sideways in the crook of his arm until he had an armload, then made his way down the row to dump it into the wheelbarrow before ducking his head and returning for more.

Rachel was also in the corn patch, a navy-blue kerchief tied over her hair, secured in the back with a firm knot. She worked fast, her face already beaded with sweat. Lucky sat at the end of the row, his wide thick tongue protruding, panting in the morning heat.

In the kitchen, the girls were washing the breakfast dishes, sweeping the kitchen, setting the house to order. No matter what the job of the day would be, Rachel never started a day's work without the kitchen being in perfect neat-as-a-pin condition.

"You can't work in chaos," she'd say. "A *huddlich* kitchen makes the whole day *huddlich*."

They sat beneath the shade of two maple trees in the backyard, on the metal porch chairs that bobbed up and down like a rocking chair. Henry sat on the edge, so he could pull off the husks in a fast downward motion and brush the silk off an ear before reaching for another one.

Lucky lay panting in the shade, sprawled out on his side, already uncomfortable in the heat.

"Poor Lucky," Rachel observed.

Henry nodded.

"You know his breed comes from a colder climate. Bennie said he's a Newfoundland."

"A what?" Rachel asked, smiling.

Henry grinned, nodding. "The place his type of dog originates from is closer to the Arctic. Bennie showed me on the map, at school."

"Really?"

"That's what he said."

Rachel smiled again, then watched Henry, already showing signs of adolescence, his shoulders widening, growing tall, perhaps a bit of fuzz above his upper lip. Those eyes, she thought, swallowing a quick rise of emotion. Dark brown pools of so much sadness. The slight variation, the turning in of one dark pupil, only added to the picture of being wizened, experienced in years far beyond his actual age. Rachel felt a quick throb of sympathy. She wanted to be closer to him, allowing him an outlet for the pain that must be spreading through him like a dark mass, shutting out the normal lively exuberance of a young boy.

How was he expected to trust in future relationships? So much had been taken from him at such a tender age.

"Henry," she began.

Immediately, his eyes focused on hers, too alert, too defiant.

"I know it's hard for you to talk about what happened to Harvey, but I worry. I want you to know that I'm here for you if you ever need to talk. Surely you must question God, why He allowed this to happen."

For a long moment, there was no response. Just when Rachel was afraid she had spoken out of turn, or words that were hurtful, cutting like knives, he took a deep breath and looked out across the yard, to the vegetable patch.

"Yeah, well." He stopped, grabbed an ear of corn, and began to husk it, tearing at the leaves as if his words could be distributed by his furious work.

Suddenly, he stopped. "I hate the creek."

Rachel watched his face and stayed quiet.

"I hate that awful brown water. It seems as if God wasn't the one who caused the creek to flood."

For a long time, Henry sat, his elbows on his knees, his hands hanging loosely between them, his head bent, so that Rachel could only see the top of his head, the wavy, loose curls, brown shot through with blond highlights.

There was a terrible light in his eyes when he fastened them on Rachel.

"Does the devil have enough power to flood a creek?"

"Oh, no. No. God is the ultimate power. The devil can only antagonize us, and if we're believers, he has no power to harm us."

"Is that true?" Henry asked, hungrily.

"Yes."

"Well, then, if God flooded the creek, why didn't He keep Harvey?"

"God has reasons, Henry. His ways are so much higher than our own, we can't even begin to understand. We don't lean on our own wisdom. God saw the big picture, the reason why He allowed this to happen. Someday, we'll look back, and we'll see it. But for now, we have to accept it and depend on our faith. You know that faith is believing, even if we don't understand? Don't you?"

"Sort of."

He sighed, a long, slow expulsion of breath that seemed world-weary.

"I thought, though, that God makes a way if we have to suffer. I heard that in church. Actually, at the funeral. So that is why I have Lucky. He takes out a lot of the missing of Harvey. Did you know he misses Harvey too?"

"No, I didn't know that."

"He does. When we go to the creek, he whimpers. He makes sounds as if he's waiting on Harvey."

And then his face crumpled, he slid off the metal chair, folded himself in a fetal position, and with both hands over his face, he shook with sobs.

Instantly, Rachel's own tears welled up, ran down her cheeks, and dripped onto her dress front.

When Malinda stalked out of the house toward them, Rachel gathered herself together, sent her back to the house to start a fire in the *kesslehaus* to heat the water.

After that day, Henry began to call her Mam. He never reverted to the old way of using her given name.

For Christmas that year, he received a new fishing pole with a reel, and a small canvas sack containing hooks and bobbers. His eyes shone with the joy of this precious gift.

Lucky and Henry roamed the fields and forests of the surrounding countryside, in every season. They knew where the ten-point buck lay, his heavy white antlers held so still they blended in with the briars and tree branches and yellow grass. They recognized which groundhog would go into which hole in the side of the alfalfa field, the outcrop of gray limestone where black snakes slithered across on their way to the creek. Chipmunks and squirrels became bold in their presence, chittering and chirring at them from fallen logs and tree branches. They knew which rafter contained the barn owl's nest, and when the young owls hatched. They recognized the difference between a raven and a crow's harsh call.

Henry would ride the harrow, bouncing along on the uneven ground behind the faithful Belgians, Sam and Bob, their heads bobbing up and down with the placing of their gigantic hooves. He knew the call of the meadowlark and the flicker, and he knew which bird had red feathers on its underside.

Everywhere Lucky and Henry went, people knew who they were, waved, called out a greeting, smiled, and shook their heads at the wonder of this lone boy's survival. He seemed able to rise above circumstance and place his future in God's hands at such a young age.

Rachel alone knew how much agony he had survived, but she kept these things in her heart. She believed Lucky was sent from God, an angel in canine form, to look after the brokenhearted twin.

But she never said anything.

The summer Henry turned fourteen years old, he became quite skilled with the new rod and reel. He lived to go fishing, the art of perfecting the perfect cast taking up much of his thoughts and all of his free time. He lived by the pond or down at the creek, him and Lucky, when the work was done and Ephraim said he could go.

An afternoon off was a rare thing, but this afternoon they had finished the last five acres of alfalfa, closed the barn door, and Ephraim smiled, shook his head, and said, yes, he could go, before Henry asked.

Henry laughed out loud, said, "Thanks, Dat," and raced off to the *kesslehaus* for his rod and reel.

Lucky bobbed up and down, bounced around on his front feet with his backside in the air, his tail waving frantically, the way he always did when he knew they were going fishing.

As they dug worms out of the manure pile behind the horse barn, Henry sang.

Oh, Lucky, we're lucky.

We're so very lucky.

My lucky old Lucky.

It was a song he often whistled under his breath, to a tune he'd made up in his mind, and Lucky liked it so much he smiled the whole time Henry sang the song.

Tonight it wasn't so hot. There was a whisper of a breeze, one that ruffled the cattail leaves, swayed the tall grasses at the edge of the pond. Dragonflies hovered over the water and mosquitoes. There was a dark brown movement on the opposite bank, then a few silent ripples spread out across the surface of the water, so Henry knew another muskrat had slid into the pond from his den in the bank.

He grabbed a fat night crawler from the tin can filled with soil and baited his hook. Then, taking a deep breath, he tried to perfect his stance, placing his front foot firmly against a tuft of grass, lifted the rod carefully behind his back, and swung with both arms.

The reel sang as the rod released the spooled line, a sound that was like music to Henry's ears. The thrill of landing a squirming night crawler in the intended spot was just so, well, he could hardly explain it, not even to himself. Fishing was something you couldn't tell other people, same as Harvey's drowning. Some things you felt in the heart, closed the door, and kept them there. It wasn't important that anyone else would know about it.

Tonight, he was sleepy. His eyes were heavy as he sat down on the pond bank. Nothing at all was happening, not even a ripple, not the slightest indication of a nibble, nothing. The sun warm on his back, Henry lay back, threw an arm across his eyes, the fishing rod propped up on a stump. A few deep breaths, and Henry was asleep, the deep sleep of the young and active.

He awoke, alarmed by an unknown thought or presence. He blinked in the fading light of the evening sun to find Katie peering into his face with an annoyed expression.

"You better come home if you're going to sleep," she said gruffly.

Henry sat up, wiped the sleep from his eyes with the back of his hand, glanced at his fishing rod that had slid off its prop, and grinned.

"Must have fallen asleep," he said wryly.

"You must have. You can't catch fish like that."

"How do you know? You don't fish."

"I would, if someone would teach me."

"Someone? Me?"

Katie nodded.

Henry looked at her, checking for sincerity.

It was there, in her serious green eyes that slanted up at the corners, surrounded by thick lashes and eyebrows that looked like a high-flying crow turned away from you.

Henry's brown eyes stayed on hers for a while, till he thought he recognized something he hadn't known he missed. It was hard to explain in words, so, of course, he didn't try to say anything to Katie after they looked at each other for so long. But he knew he had discovered a feeling. Was it friendship? Sibling recognition? He just knew that her eyes were green, shot through with brown and gold lines, like the water behind the biggest limestone on Pequea Creek, and that he needed to see those eyes more than once.

Katie was short for a fifteen-year-old. Short and a bit plump, not much, but soft like a marshmallow. She looked like a pillow in some parts of her, which was nice.

When he talked again, his voice shook until he steadied it. He had to do something with his hands so he wouldn't keep looking for those brown and gold lights in her green eyes.

"So if you want to learn to fish, you'll need a pole."

He held up his rod and reel.

"I know. I don't have one."

"Ephraim got me this one."

Katie sat down on the thick green grass, pulled off a long blade, and wound it around her forefinger.

Henry watched as she pulled it tight, the tip of her finger turned red.

"Your finger's going to fall off, you keep that up."

"You think?"

Henry nodded.

"Don't you ever say Dat, for Ephraim?"

"Sometimes."

"Doesn't he seem like your father, after, what is it? Seven years? Eight?"

Henry wound another night crawler on his hook. Katie leaned over and watched.

"Eight years, I guess," Henry said, after a while.

"So Dat doesn't seem like your father."

"In some ways. But I'll always know he's not my real father."

"Yeah. Guess so."

A comfortable silence hung between them, while Henry straightened, twisted his body, and cast perfectly into the middle of the pond with a soft splooshing sound. The red-and-white bobbin floated on the surface.

"Are you going to teach me how to do that?" Katie asked.

"I can if you want."

"I do."

"All right."

"Don't I seem like your sister, either?" Katie asked in a small voice.

Henry shrugged.

"What does that mean?" she persisted.

"Well, you're just Katie. I mean, I like you, of course, but no, you're not my sister."

"Now you're hurting my feelings."

"I don't mean to. Here, now hold the rod with this hand, here. Then, place your other hand on the handle."

"Like this?"

"No. You have to put your right hand higher on the pole, like this."

Henry stood behind her, took her hand and placed it in the proper position.

"Now, bring the whole rod back with both hands, like this. Then, let fly. Concentrate on zinging that hook as far as you can."

Katie leaned back into his chest.

Her white covering smelled like starch and flowers. She smelled like the sun on wet grass, and the rose by the porch early in the morning when the dew sat on the yellow petals before the sun was finished rising above the north pasture. When she stepped forward and away from him, he wished she wouldn't have.

This was not good. This was certainly not how a person was supposed to feel about his sister. But she wasn't his sister at all. Henry didn't really know what to do with this unreasonable, misunderstood craziness.

Better to act as if nothing had changed. It hadn't; not really.

Katie laughed, a high, tinkling sound that carried across the pond. "Look at that. Barely away from the bank."

"It's okay, for the first try," Henry said gruffly.

They stayed by the pond till the sky turned from pink and lavender streaks to a night sky. Bullfrogs chugged from their hidden alcoves among the rushes, the nighttime insect choir began in earnest. Both of them caught bluegills and sunfish, put them in on a stringer, and hung it from a tree root.

They sat side by side, Lucky on Henry's side. They didn't know they were reluctant to return home, but they were. It was so peaceful, so filled with sounds of the pond, the water lapping gently between the thick rushes.

"Should we go back?" Katie asked.

"Guess so."

They gathered up the stringer of fish, the bait can, and walked slowly along the cow path that led to the farm, the barn and house merely a silhouette with tiny white stars pricking through the darkening sky. There was a kinship between them now, the love of fishing, the mutual understanding that they both had something to look forward to.

Rachel was delighted with the fish. She told Henry to clean them, and she'd roll them in flour and fry them in lard. They'd have a bedtime snack.

Katie wanted to learn how to filet the fish, so with Anna following after them, Henry washed, gutted, beheaded, and cut the thin filets from the sides.

Anna stuck her nose in the air like a hound dog ready to howl at the moon, saying fish smelled worse than cow patties, then left them to finish the job by lantern light.

Henry laughed and asked Katie if she thought these fish smelled bad.

She looked at Henry's dark brown eyes in the yellow glow of the lantern and said, of course not.

Henry smiled at her, and she smiled back at him, and he felt as if some of the ache of missing Harvey had been erased by a soft, kind eraser. Not all of it, he hadn't planned on going through life without it, of course, but it was as if the part that hurt the most had somehow been erased.

# Chapter Six

THAT WAS THE BEGINNING.

It was the start of something new. It brought a light into Henry's life that made his world different, thinking of quiet Katie as a companion for both himself and Lucky.

Lucky was getting old now. There were white hairs on his chest and below his jaw, and he no longer bounced on his front legs with his backside in the air. He walked steadily, in places where he used to run. He no longer catapulted himself into the pond from a perfect standstill, either. He still accompanied Henry everywhere he went. Henry still put both arms around the big shaggy dog's neck, laid his head on his back, and cried when missing Harvey became as heavy as a stone in his chest. No one else understood. No one else sat quietly and knew what he was feeling except Lucky.

The change was not about the dog, his faithful friend. It was the glimpse of a life where there was the reality of something greater than missing Harvey. It was even different than knowing about God.

When Henry had times in his life when the pain became unbearable, he had often felt a caring, like a soft whoosh of breath. At night, alone in the double bed, when he remembered that Harvey would never come back, he shuddered with sobs that came from deep within the stone of pain, smashing his resolve into a thousand pieces.

Usually, when those times came, it was followed by the absolute knowing, the recognizing of God's love and His caring about the missing of Harvey. Sometimes, Henry thought the comfort might be angels, *die engel*, he heard about in church, the angels Ephraim talked about in his evening prayer. He believed in angels. He believed they watched over him, and that they were sent by God. His faith had no beginning and no end. He could never tell where it started. He just knew that he had always been aware of heavenly beings.

These angels had certainly been there when he and Harvey walked side by side down the road to spend the rest of their lives with Ephraim and Rachel.

Harvey had argued with him, when he mentioned this. It was funny about Katie, the way he never noticed her much. Malinda was there, loud and bossy, someone to be reckoned with, and Anna was the playful one, who spent more time with the twins than anyone else. Katie never said much.

Harvey said once that she was someone who was afraid of her own shadow.

Not now she wasn't.

She was a good fisher person.

Till autumn's cool breath chased away summer's stifling heat, she had acquired the art of perfect casting. That was when they became competitive, battling to the finish to see who could catch the most, the biggest, the best.

Henry admired her. His admiration changed to awe when she used cheese on her hook and landed the largest, fattest small-mouth bass Henry had ever seen.

He laughed at her for putting cheese on her hook.

"You wait, Henry Esh," she said. "You wait. Fish have a keen sense of smell, you know."

That fat bass measured twenty-one inches and was full of clumps of roe. Katie fought the fish as it leaped and dived, giving the line just enough slack to let the great fish wear itself out fighting that hook. When her arms became tired with the effort, Henry offered to take over, but she set her jaw, shook her head, and fought on.

Henry cheered, yelling from the stump he stood on, calling directions, which she mostly ignored. Finally, she told him to get down off that stump and quit yelling, so Henry did, but only because she wanted him to.

They caught so many fish, Rachel had to put them on ice in the icebox. They had fish for dinner, fish for supper. They ate fish soup and broiled fish with potatoes and parsley.

Finally, Rachel threw up her hands and asked them to take the heavy stringer full of fish to Henry's parents. They would appreciate a fine meal of fish, she said. Henry looked at Katie, doubt clouding his brown eyes.

The times he had returned to his home were often awkward. It was like being told to turn left and you knew you'd gone right, but it was too late to fix the situation, so you just kept going, blindly, dumbly, as if you could never quite grasp the reason. Like chasing a ball of dandelion seeds that poofed into nothing before you knew it.

It always left Henry feeling inadequate, empty, wrapped in a veil of thin, gauzy guilt that trapped him. He didn't want Katie to see his own family. He told her to stay, he'd go.

"I want to go," she said.

"I don't want you to."

"Why not?"

"Oh, just . . . I don't know."

"C'mon, Henry."

"All right. But, well . . . You see, Katie, I'm ashamed they're my family. They are so terrible poor."

"It doesn't matter."

He looked down at her, allowed himself the pleasure of meeting all those yellow and gold lights that danced in her green eyes.

"Thanks, Katie."

"You're welcome."

He smiled at her, a smile that appeared infrequently. A smile that changed those sad brown eyes for only an instant.

They took the wagon, laid a burlap bag on the bed, then put the fish along the center.

Henry pulled the wagon, with Katie at his side, Lucky walking ahead, the great paws moving in a steady rhythm.

It was a brisk, chilly evening, with the gold of maple leaves setting off the burnt orange of the pin oaks, and the bright October sky showing signs of an overcast tomorrow. Instead of a red sunset, there was a line of gray clouds rising in the west.

"Rain coming," Henry observed.

Katie looked up, nodded.

"Want me to pull awhile?"

"No."

"Tell me, Henry, how does it make you feel when you go home? Don't you wish they would have kept you?"

"I don't know." Henry shrugged his shoulders. "It's hard to explain. I . . . ah, I don't know."

"Tell me, Henry, I'll just listen."

"Nothing."

"Oh, c'mon."

"It's just hard to imagine having been raised there. If I think on it too much, it doesn't get me anywhere.

My life is what it is now, so I'll go forward. I mean, I feel like I should love my family, but I hardly know them. I remember feeling ashamed of their . . . their being so poor, in school, in church. And a guilty feeling, I guess, that we have more."

"But you shouldn't be guilty. They gave you away. It wasn't that you asked to go."

"You're right, I guess."

"You haven't had an easy life, Henry."

Henry had nothing to say to this. He looked at Katie, and she looked at him. They said nothing.

The driveway was pocked with puddles, icelike pieces of organdy along the edges. Brown weeds hung over the fence like forgotten slivers of summer's growth, the boards loosened and sagging from post to post. Skinny mules with sides like washboards, their large heads too long and bony to support their monstrous ears, eyed them without interest, the only movement an occasional flap of their lower lip. A few razor-thin barn cats skittered ahead of them, their thin tails held aloft like handles. The deep baying of a coon hound erupted, shattering the crisp, evening air.

Lucky stopped, his ears pressed forward.

"S'all right, Lucky."

Henry's hand spread out on the dog's massive head. Katie moved closer to Henry, placed her hand beside his on the handle of the wagon.

Loose barn doors creaked on the evening breeze. The yard gate squeaked as they pushed it open and made their way up the dirt path to the door. Henry waited, collecting himself, breathing lightly to avoid the smell of sour milk and cow manure that clung to the row of rubber Tingly boots strewn across the porch. The screen door had only one corner of the screen intact, the rest of it hung loose, flapping in the breeze.

When Henry knocked, there was a scuffling from inside before Rueben Esh came to the door, pulling it open slowly, then peering around it, taking a considerable amount of time to say hello, as if he couldn't remember who this tall young man was.

"Oh, it's Henry," he said slowly.

"Hello, Dat."

"Come in."

Together, they stepped inside, with the string of fish held up for everyone to see. Children of various ages, dressed in the same shade of faded cotton, grouped quietly, without uttering any opinion or exclamation. Mattie came from the bedroom, paused, threw her hands up.

"Why, Henry! A surprise that you came by. Who caught all the fish?"

"We did. Me and Katie."

Mattie's eyes narrowed as she looked the young girl up and down, taking in the large eyes, the clean, gleaming hair, the heart-shaped face, the dress made out of *Ordnung*. Too short. Here was a girl who was not for Henry. What were those Ephraim Stoltzfus' thinking, allowing their daughter to traipse around the roads in broad daylight? They were no longer children.

What if Bishop David came along in his buggy and saw them pulling that wagon?

So she frowned, took the fish off the stringer without speaking. Rueben asked Henry about his health, if Ephraim had the corn fodder all in, if the cows were milking good, which Henry answered in polite sentences.

Mattie turned from the sink with the empty stringer, appraised Katie with a knowing look, and without preamble, inquired about her age.

Katie too answered politely.

Well, thought Mattie, she'll be with the *rumschp-ringa* soon enough, Henry won't have a chance. After this thought entered her head, her smile returned to her face, and she became friendly, keeping up a volley of questions Henry answered dutifully.

When Henry left, Mattie had a spring in her step. Yes, Henry was a handsome young man, well spoken, and well raised. He had nothing to do with Rueben's lack of interest in work or getting ahead. He would amount to something. And the way he bent his straw hat. Down in front and back, so neat, and such a frame for that square jaw and brown eyes. His voice had changed, lowered, to a manly growl.

Yes, Mattie was glad he had been raised by Ephraim and Rachel. He had learned Ephraim's ways of farming, to get up at 4:30 in the morning and finish all the chores before breakfast, the way her own father taught them. And still she loved her Rueben, tuned in to his lack of ambition and accepted him for what he was, creating an aura of peace and honor in the children as well.

But things were tucked away in the recesses of her heart. Thoughts about life, things no one else would ever know. It kept the days bearable, providing joy in the midst of the life-straining poverty.

Henry and Katie walked quietly, pulling the empty wagon, their hands side by side on the handle, Lucky walking close to Henry, a hand resting on his back.

"They seem nice to you, Henry," Katie observed.

"They are."

Henry had seen the narrow appraisal of Katie and the light of pride in Mattie's eyes. She was a true mother, in a sense, and he hoped someday, after he was married, with children of his own, he could visit more often and become a part of her life. But he said nothing to Katie.

"Henry, I'll be joining the *youngie* in the spring."

"I know."

"Before you know it, I'll be married, and then who will fish with you?"

"Anna?"

"Anna! Don't you know how she hates to fish?"

"No."

"She would never bait a hook or pull off a fish."

"Well, then, perhaps I'll just go back to me and Lucky."

"Would you rather?"

Henry considered her question. They both felt the bump and tug as Lucky leaped silently onto the wagon, and sat proudly, his mouth wide, laughing at them.

"Lucky!"

Henry burst out laughing, then let Katie hold the wagon handle while he went to throw his arms around his pet.

"You're tired, Lucky, you old white-haired dog," he laughed. Katie laughed with him.

"He's smart."

"He sure is. All right, Lucky, we'll pull you on home."

"You didn't answer my question," Katie said.

"What?"

"Would you rather go fishing without me?"

"No. Of course not."

"Do you enjoy when I go fishing with you?"

"That's a dumb question. Of course I do."

Katie smiled.

"I guess that means we're fishing buddies."

"It does."

In companionable silence, they turned in the long driveway to the farm, set against the backdrop of brilliant fall foliage and brown squares of land, green squares of fall-seeded rye like a patchwork quilt, the white buildings cast in a golden glow of sunset. The black-and-white Holsteins munched the pasture grass contentedly, the Belgians hung their massive heads over the top rail of the board fence, the white-painted fence that never had a loose nail or a broken board. The barn roof had just been given a fresh coat of silver paint, the garden was cleaned and seeded with rye grass and a good cover of manure. Firewood was stacked as high as a man's head in the woodshed, the cellar was full of fruits and vegetables in gleaming mason jars, the potato bin overflowing with large brown potatoes covered with the fine dust, all that remained of the fertile soil that had been their home all summer long.

Henry felt the blessing. It seeped into a part of his heart and stayed there. He turned to Katie.

"When you're with the *youngie*, will you no longer go fishing?"

"I don't know. Do people change so much after they are *rumschpringa* that they no longer do the things they did growing up, like fishing and sledding?"

Henry shrugged. "I guess that would be up to each person."

"Right. Well, we'll see how it goes."

Lucky leaped off the wagon, jerking the handle.

"Lucky! You just decide yourself when it's time to get off," Katie said, laughing.

"He does what he wants. He's my best friend."

"Better than me?" Katie inquired.

"Lucky was there for me through . . . through all of it."

"And I wasn't?"

"No, not really. I hardly knew you. You were just one of the girls. Malinda, Katie, Anna. All the same to me."

"Now I'm not all the same?"

"Well, no, not really. I mean, we fish and talk. A lot, actually."

"So I'm a special friend? Like Lucky?"

"Yes."

"Good."

"But that will change in the spring when you turn sixteen."

"Why does it have to?"

"You'll be, well, asked."

"Asked?"

"You know what I mean."

"It doesn't matter if I'm asked, if I don't like the person who's asking."

"That's true."

They stood by the yard gate, the sun sliding behind the horizon, casting them in the deepening twilight. A hawk soared close above the treetops, sounding its loud screech, sending a volley of frightened house sparrows spraying through the yellowing leaves like gunshot.

Ephraim came walking up to them, his shoulders hunched, hands in his pockets, the way he walked when he was tired. How well Henry knew him, this adopted father. And loved him. Yes, he did love him. Always glad to see him in the morning, grinning at him as he sat on his milking stool, with his wide smile, saying "*Guta mya.*" Anger was rare, and if he was seen in a display of displeasure, it was not the fearful kind, where your mouth turned dry and your heart went galloping in your chest.

Henry thought often on the salt of the earth. He believed Ephraim was a very large jar of salt of the earth, the real kind, the kind that was sprinkled all over the farm, flavoring life for his wife and children, his animals and fields, all his neighbors, English and Mennonite and Amish, plus every person in the church. Ephraim had a flavorful attitude toward his neighbor, anyone he came to know. His friends multiplied each year, his easy chuckle and conversation like a magnet to the milkman, the feed man, the fertilizer salesman. Henry absorbed all these things as he lived among the good attitude, the benevolence with which Ephraim lived his life.

Two Christmases came and went. Two years of absorbing Ephraim and Rachel's ways, learning about the good management of the farm, what made the cows produce record amounts of milk, which lime or fertilizer was needed and when to apply it.

Nothing was wasted, nothing squandered for pleasure. And yet, his adoptive parents were not stingy,

always generous with the children's needs, remembering birthdays with a homemade cake and presents
wrapped in paper.

Henry turned seventeen, became a member of the
Amish church through a summer of instruction class-
es and baptism. He had no earth-shaking experience,
no testimony about the new birth, and no idea how
he would go about describing it. But it was there.

God had always been there.

He had always believed that when Jesus died on
the cross, He rose out of the grave, defied the power
of death and hell, so now this grace was sufficient for
him. It had taken Harvey to Heaven, and someday,
when God chose, Henry would join him there.

Heaven, angels, God, Jesus, the Holy Ghost, all of
it was very real to Henry, and he just always figured
that on account of Harvey's drowning, a part of him
already was in Heaven.

When he turned sixteen years of age and began
his *rumschpringa*, he was tempted same as everyone
else—the wild girls and the drinking of alcoholic
beverages and cigarette smoking. It was enticing, ex-
citing, forbidden fruit that he did not always resist.

But it held no real thrill. It was an illusion of happiness. It left him empty and ashamed of himself. Heaven and God moved away during that time. Later, he knew it wasn't that God went anywhere. God stayed the same. It was Henry who moved away, drawn by the beckoning finger of cheap thrills and hidden sins.

Katie began to date a young man from New Holland, Benuel Fisher, who was a lot older. Henry thought he might be twenty-three years old.

Henry didn't want Katie to be dating Benuel, but hardly knew what to do about it. He was just a young *schpritza* and not even half good enough for her. Malinda was married now, and Anna turned sixteen that winter, so Henry never considered himself good enough for any of them. Not that he considered Malinda.

She was still as bossy and overbearing as ever. She had better count herself lucky to have a husband at all, the poor string bean Davey King, tall and skinny and obedient. Henry figured the marriage would go well; he would obey while she led.

He felt regret, though, about Katie. He believed he loved her when she was fifteen, the way he loved looking into her eyes. But he was younger, only fourteen years old, and when she was with the *youngie*, she was always being asked for a date with Elam or Abner or Rueben or Enos.

So Henry gave up.

He actually asked God to give him Katie, at first, but that didn't happen. So he swallowed his misery and tried to become interested in Rhoda, but she was too vain and made him feel like a schoolboy who kept repeating the wrong answers to a disapproving teacher.

Through these years, Henry still had Lucky. Old and grizzled now, stiff in every joint, half-blind and arthritic, he still followed Henry around the farm. He still rose from his bed in the forebay of the barn, stretched, his mouth wide in the dog smile, then walked painfully to greet Henry, who always fell on his knees to caress and murmur, to stroke and love his beloved friend.

# Chapter Seven

THE SNOWS CAME EARLY AT CHRISTMAS IN 1940. A foot of it fell the day before, followed by a stiff wind that sent billows of it rolling across fields and roads of Lancaster County. The cold deepened, buoyed by Arctic air that came down from Canada, riding on the wind.

Henry was twenty-one now, the age when he was a man. He kept his own wages and decided his course through life. Tall, with the same wavy brown hair and sad brown eyes, he received a good pay from Ephraim now, who counted Henry as a hired hand, worthy of a steady wage each month.

Henry was at an important crossroad in his life. He felt the need for a lifelong companion, a good wife at his side as he began his own life of farming. He simply didn't know who to ask.

Katie had married Benuel Fisher in 1937, when Henry was almost nineteen. He had been in the bridal party in the honored tradition of *nava-sitza*, trying hard to congratulate the couple. Pushing back thoughts of being seated across the corner table with Katie as his rightful wife, he watched her glowing face as she went through her wedding day dressed in navy blue with a crisp white organdy cape and apron pinned to her small waist.

He didn't sleep much the night after the wedding. He thought of Christ in Gethsemane and knew He suffered unbelievably; so this was only a blip, a minor thing.

Till it wasn't.

Waves of longing, memories of the sun shining on her face, her eyes flashing green and gold lights, her perfect mouth wide as she laughed, landing a large-mouth bass yet again. Katie at the wash line, singing her silly songs. Katie scrubbing the kitchen floor, sitting up, yelling at him to get off that wet floor. Katie permeated his thoughts like a heady scent of lavender or roses, lived in every waking hour.

It was in 1940 when he came out to the barn to find Lucky stiff and cold, lying in his doghouse, on a fresh bed of straw. Henry had spread it with care, extra thick, knowing Lucky's joints ached, especially in winter, when the cold crept around the building and seeped into every available crevice.

Outside, the wind roared, smacked against the barn windows like a giant hand, sending a blinding wall of snow across the barnyard. Tears blinded his vision as he drew Lucky from his doghouse and stroked the great, cold head one last time.

*Ach*, Lucky. Lucky.

Two losses, now. Harvey and Lucky.

And yes, Katie.

Today at the Christmas dinner, there would be Katie.

He watched the numbing snow, the bending of the bare, black branches of the maple tree, whipping back and forth in the grip of the frenzied wind.

He looked down at Lucky.

He had so much with this big, shaggy dog. A real companion. A faithful friend who absorbed all his childhood sorrows and gave back all the love and support he needed. But now he had gone the way of all animals, all humans. Eventually, life came to an end for every living creature on the face of the earth.

The incredible part was that God knew everything, even the fall of a sparrow, and now, of Lucky.

God had stilled the stout heart. It was time for Lucky to go, leaving Henry with an endless stream of warm memories that became a part of who he was.

Another dog?

Not for now.

Ephraim came to see Henry bent over the form of his dog. He clapped a sympathetic hand on his shoulder and said, "Poor old dog." He left Henry to grieve.

They debated the wisdom of setting off for the Beiler Christmas dinner that day, Rachel saying rather than risk a life, they were best off at home. Ephraim took note of the edge of seriousness in his intuitive wife and agreed. They said it was up to Henry if he wanted to attempt the trip, but in these conditions, they may become stranded.

So he agreed, beset the way he was by a sense of melancholy. He laid Lucky on a canvas tarp and dragged him to the implement shed and buried him beneath the wagon, where there was no snow.

It was hard work, but it buoyed his flagging spirits. Outside, the wind increased as the day wore on, turning eastern Pennsylvania and parts of Maryland and Virginia into a howling maelstrom of wind, snow, and ice.

They did not receive the news till Monday morning, the roads impassable by the strength of the blizzard. A snowplow hit Benuel and Katie on their way home from the Christmas dinner, killing the horse and Benuel, hitting the left side of the buggy as they made a right-hand turn, a wall of blowing snow evidently blinding Benuel as he turned.

Katie and the baby were in critical condition in Lancaster at the hospital.

Henry received the news with only a slight lowering of his eyelids, his jaw clenched, square and hard. Muscles in his cheek worked as he tried to contain the news that roared in his head.

How critical?

She would die with her husband.

The baby. What was his name? John. Jonathan. Yoni.

He couldn't think.

Turning, he made his way upstairs, blindly sought the door of his room, sat on the edge of his bed, shook like an oak leaf in a summer storm. His teeth rattled in his mouth. His hand went up to still the trembling. He felt as if he was in the grip of a gigantic beast that needed to devour him, finish him off, fling him aside like a torn rag doll with no life, no flesh and blood.

What was this?

Did God forget mercy where Henry was concerned? What was God's will? How could he know?

He stayed, the edge of his bed holding him up. He shivered and became numb with the cold of the unheated upstairs of the farmhouse.

Ephraim and Rachel left, he could hear them following the town police to their car. Anna was left alone.

Better go down to her, poor thing.

He gathered himself to go downstairs, to find Anna curled on the old davenport in the kitchen, weeping softly. He stood close to the distraught young woman, feeling clumsy, ill at ease, and he didn't know what to do with his hands.

"Are you all right, Anna?" he croaked hoarsely.

She sat up.

He saw the need for a handkerchief and provided it. She looked at him, said, *Denke.*

He sat down on the opposite side of the couch and stared at his white-stockinged feet. He didn't know what to say.

Finally, when the loud ticking of the clock became unbearable, he rose, checked the fire in the kitchen range, went to the *kesslehaus* for small pieces of wood, stoked the red embers until a flame arose, then replaced the lid. He stood at the kitchen sink, gripped the edges until his knuckles turned white, watching the wind's half-hearted attempt at blowing the edges of the crested snowdrifts. The sun was brilliant, casting blue swirls of color in the pristine landscape, where the hollows created shadows. Pine trees swayed in triumph, waving green banners of bare branches the wind had freed from their load of snow.

Grace and mercy, grace and mercy, tumbled through his mind. Spare Katie, dear God. You know I have loved her. Have always loved her. I love her still.

And now, if she lived, he would have another chance. But he should absolutely not think this thought. Selfish. Unholy. Profane.

Forgive me.

He felt Anna's presence, a cooling shadow to his fevered thoughts. She placed a hand on his arm, where the long sleeves were rolled up, halfway on his thick forearms. Her fingers were small, white, and tapered, as soft as a snow bunting on a winter snowdrift.

"Could you just hold me for a minute?" she whispered.

Henry started. He looked down at her. Yes, down. She was so tiny, so blonde.

"You mean . . . ?"

Henry had never held a girl in his arms. When other young men had taken the "wild" girls for a fling, he had always held back.

For an answer, she stepped close, put her small arms around his waist, laid her head on his chest, and wept softly, a womanly sound of grief that was unbearable.

Henry couldn't hear it.

He folded his strong, young arms around this slight girl and held her. Strong emotion welled up, feelings he could not decipher. He wanted to keep Anna there, where she was, till the end of time.

Mentally, he shook himself. He was distraught, that was all. Anna was nothing to him, and never would be. It was Katie he loved.

Too soon, she sighed, stepped back, her head bent.

"I'm sorry," she whispered.

"Don't be. It's all right."

Almost, he pulled her close, but she looked up. Her eyes were red from weeping, but they were very blue, the blinding light of the sun on the snow revealing silver lights like music notes of feeling in their depths.

Henry was shaken, unable to tear his own eyes from hers. His hands hung clumsily at his sides, the world spun sideways, then righted itself. He heard the clock's loud ticking, winced when it slammed out the hour in its tinny crescendo.

He swallowed, slowed his breathing.

"I'm sorry about Lucky," she said, soft and low.

Henry could only nod and watch her face. Skin like a porcelain doll, a nose so perfect, and full lips.

He tore himself away, shrugged into his coat, slapped his hat on his head, and went to the barn, fast, without looking back. He had a childish longing to turn around, to see if she stood at the window now, watching him. He wanted to wave, smile, shout, and skip the rest of the way to the barn.

He fed horses, swept the aisles, fed the heifers without ridding himself of her.

Anna!

Little Anna. He had never thought of her, much less noticed her. She never said anything. Not to him, hardly ever.

He reasoned himself into sensible plateaus, high places of rationality he could view from a firm footing, alone in the barn. Lucky dead, which had served to weaken his resolve, his best ability to stay strong. The tragic news, his thoughts running ahead of God's ways.

Anna meant nothing. She was only seeking comfort. She had not tried to convey anything other than that. It was all his runaway emotion at a time when defenses were down.


Ephraim and Rachel returned late that night, after Henry and Anna had done chores together, awkwardly, silently, giving each other a wide berth.

Katie entered into her rest less than a week later, the baby the only survivor.

Little Yonie, not yet a year old.

It was a time of darkness for Henry, a time when he moved through the valley of the shadow of death in the truest sense of the verse. He could not regain his footing, no matter how valiantly he struggled. Anger, questions, frustrations, the inability to accept her death, raged within him like a storm, obscuring the way, hurling him into an outer darkness that felt as he imagined hell to be.

He lost weight, his face grew pale, with ever increasing circles darkening beneath his eyes.

He didn't have Lucky.

Ephraim scoured the countryside for a Newfoundland. Would have paid an exorbitant price. Rachel cooked his favorite dishes. Anna returned to her former shadowy self.

They took in the baby Yonie, of course. Their son, their grandson, whose roly-poly little body had the power to erase the worst of their grief. A happy baby, chortling over the wonders of a spool of thread or a wooden block.

Spring came early.

The earth exploded with color and scent, as wild strawberry blooms, purple violets, and buttered yellow dandelions pranced onstage, showing their ability to cheer even the most downhearted. Bluebirds appeared on fenceposts, trilling their beautiful song, woodpeckers pounded the trunks of trees like accompanying drums.

Life resumed its normality. Henry plowed the north lot, turning over the rich black soil like a row of giant worms, then bounced over them with the disc and the harrow, the squeaking of leather harness in tune with the thumping of the steel teeth that tore into the soil.

He thought he saw a coyote, at first. No, he decided, a fox. Too big for either one. The low, bent hindquarters. Triangles for ears.

A German shepherd.

He stopped the team. Crouched down and snapped his fingers, calling to the dog.

That was the wrong thing. The dog planted his feet firmly, his ears like two large triangles, head up, then took off in one leap sideways, ran low and hard until he disappeared into the pine woods.

Henry shook his head, stayed on the plow, and resumed the day's work.

The sun shone overhead, the spring warmth like a comforting blanket after winter's harsh exposure. Everywhere he looked, there were marvels of creation, myriad birdsong, flocks of geese in their perfect form, honking their raucous spring cry on their way to build nests in the bulrushes by the edge of the pond.

The geese's cry was only another reminder of Katie, the way the sun caught the highlights in her hair, the way it turned her tanned face into a golden glow, her eyes alight as she expertly landed yet another fish.

Why hadn't he asked her? What had held him back, if he knew she was the one love of his life?

Cowardice. Plain old shrinking away of his own audacity to imagine she would ever come to love him.

For who was he?

A remaining twin, given away like an extra kitten, from a family wallowing in poverty. Skinny old Rueben Esh. Never amounted to a hill of beans.

That, he had overheard at an auction.

So now, would he ever amount to more?

Or would he, unknowing, become his father?

He was unworthy, still, and had been back when his love for Katie resided like a burr in his heart, uncomfortable, prickly, but unable to be removed. Thoughts were burdensome, heavy things that sat in your head with a dead weight if you allowed them to do that. Better to think thoughts of spring, the warm air, the sunshine, although, it too brought a deep longing, a cry from within, almost a painful reaching for some mysterious thing he could not name.

A bittersweet wanting, as if the past and the future were all wrapped up in one unknowable yearning.

One thing was sure: the heart must always long for God, first and foremost. One of his favorite verses in the Bible was the one about not leaning to your own understanding, but sincerely ask to be shown Thy way, direct my path.

Henry bowed his head.

Tears coursed down his face as he cried out silently, groaning from the depth of his soul, asking God to do just that.

Direct my path, show me Thy ways, O Lord.

The horses were sweating now, the white foam appearing wherever the harnesses rubbed against their bodies. Their noble heads kept bobbing, their thick muscular necks straining against their collars, and still they kept going.

Time for a break.

Henry pulled on the reins, shouted, "Whoa, whoa there, Bob," to the lead horse.

Heads lowered gratefully, strong necks distended, stretched. Nostrils dilated, their breath coming in strong puffs, their sides heaving. They rested, their faithful doelike eyes watching Henry as he flopped on his back, threw an arm across his eyes, relaxed in the fresh spring grass that grew abundantly along the edge of the field.

Every day the dog appeared, watching Henry with frightened eyes. Every day, Henry tried to befriend him, but each time, the dog leaped, panicked, and ran.

He told Ephraim about the dog, at the supper table. Ephraim shook his head, swallowed, raised a forefinger and shook it in Henry's direction.

"German shepherds aren't to be trusted."

"Especially strays," Rachel chimed in.

Anna said nothing, as usual, her head bent slightly as she buttered a homemade dinner roll.

"I can't get him to come to me, so nothing to worry about," Henry said, laughing.

"I could," Anna said, unexpectedly.

Henry looked at her, raised his eyebrows.

"How would you do that?"

She smiled. "I won't say."

Her parents watched their quiet, youngest daughter. At nineteen years of age, she showed no interest in dating, never related any of her weekend activities to her mother, went about her life in so much silence, so much solitude, that Rachel often worried.

Was there something wrong with her?

Rachel was well aware of the two grown children at the dinner table not being blood relatives at all, but as far as she could tell, they were brother and sister in the truest sense of the word. They simply lived in the same house, worked in the same fields and in the barn, barely speaking to each other.

So when Anna showed an interest in the dog, everyone was surprised, but, wisely, made no fuss.

Henry looked at her.

"Well then, if you won't say, maybe I'd better watch, so I can learn something."

"No, I don't want you to be there."

Henry nodded, raised his eyebrows, then bent to his second helping of mashed potatoes and beef gravy.

Anna ate her buttered dinner roll, and nothing more was said.

Henry forgot about Anna's words, having finished the plowing of that particular field, and starting another on the south end of the farm, closer to the pond.

The day was gray, lowering clouds bunched together as if they were conferring when to let loose the downpour that was sure to come. The air was chilly with a penetrating dampness that found its way through Henry's light denim coat.

There was movement to his left. Instantly he thought of the dog.

There.

Black, dark colors.

To his amazement, he saw first Anna, dressed in a dark scarf and black coat, her navy-blue dress mostly covered by the black apron.

Henry leaned back on the reins. "Whoa, whoa!"

By her side walked the German shepherd.

"Anna!" Henry shouted.

She put a finger to her lips. "Shhh!"

Henry remained on the plow as they approached. The dog stopped, his eyes intently rooted on Henry's face. Anna's hand went to his head, her fingers spread in much the same way Henry had always cupped the skull of the massive Lucky.

"He doesn't trust you," Anna said, her voice low and even.

Henry got off the plow, but stayed where he was.

"I can see that," he said.

It seemed like long moments, when nothing was said, the dog refusing to sit, standing alert, eyeing Henry with brown eyes, large and unfriendly. The heavy tail did not wave. Yet there was Anna, waiting without fear.

Henry watched the dog's face, the way his legs remained stiff, ready to spring.

"He doesn't like me," he said, finally.

Anna nodded.

"I think he's been mistreated, probably by a man. So I suggest we walk with him, on a leash. I'll take him back to the barn, to Luck . . . the . . . doghouse, then later, when chores are finished, we'll win you over."

That was a long speech from the quiet, unassuming Anna.

Henry watched the dog.

He was a fine specimen. A good bloodline, evidently. He was, in fact, beautiful, for a German shepherd breed. The coarse hair on the back of his neck stood up. A low rumbling came from his throat. But he stood at attention, with Anna's hand on his head.

Henry realized his holding back, the reservation with which he assessed this dog. It wasn't Lucky. The eyes were too big, protruding from his head, not small and triangular and almost buried in thick, silky, black hair. His mouth wasn't laughing, and his skin did not roll around on his enormous frame when he walked so that he seemed to frolic.

This was simply the wrong dog.

Anna saw the struggle on Henry's face.

That was all right.

She was the wrong girl too. She knew this. Always had. She turned and walked away, without a sound.

Henry went back to his plowing with a sense of defeat. What was up with Anna, anyway?

When Katie died, he had been shaken to the core with the possibility of having loved the wrong girl. Anna meant more to him than he ever thought possible.

But now, everything he'd dreamed of had died out, like an untended fire. He shrugged, lifted his face to the sky as the first raindrops began to fall, turned the team, and made his way home.

# Chapter Eight

HENRY WATCHED ANNA WITH THE DOG, watched her walk him on a leash, throw balls and sticks, watched him unleash ferocious power, gathering his hind legs under his body like a panther, his bright eyes watching every single move she made, till the ball or the stick was flung into the air in a wide arc, and he was off.

Tremendous power and speed. Agile as all get out. Henry sometimes shook his head in wonder.

But still Anna did not invite him to join. By all accounts, the dog was hers alone.

Henry went fishing by himself.

He often looked back over his shoulder, looking for Anna and the dog. He still thought she might want to join him someday, learn the art of casting the way Katie had. All through spring and now into summer, he had no reason to believe he even existed, as far as Anna was concerned.

She named the dog Colonel, pronounced like a kernel of corn, a hated word that had the upper-grade boys snickering when he pronounced it the way it was spelled.

But he had to admit it was an impressive name, given to an impressive dog. He was beautiful now, under Anna's care. She sneaked an egg from the hen-house; Henry had seen her do it.

Colonel was filled out, his coat sleek.

Henry felt pangs of unwanted jealousy.

But still she didn't invite him.

The whole thing was frustrating. She had told him that day on the plow that *they*, not just her, would walk him on a leash. And yet, he had never been asked to accompany her.

Last night on the porch swing, Anna sat on one corner, so small she hardly took up a fourth of the swing. She was wearing a pale blue dress, the color of the evening sky, and no apron, the heat hanging over the countryside till late.

She was reading, never looking up at his approach. He asked if he could sit. She barely took her eyes from the book, nodding in an absent way.

He sat on the opposite end of the swing, look-ing out over the yard and the garden, watching the shadows creep up behind the implement shed, the fireflies blinking their tiny yellow lights as darkness approached.

All was quiet from the reader.

Henry glanced her way a few times, but she was so absorbed in her book, he didn't want to disturb that concentration, the way her eyebrows were drawn down by the intensity on her face.

He breathed deeply.

She smelled like soap and flowers and the dew in the morning. Her hair was like corn silk, but shinier.

He didn't know what to do about either one, so he sighed again. He realized if he wanted to get to know this girl, he'd have to do what came so hard for him. Make advances, take the lead, talk to her, ask questions. With Katie, she had done all that. Until she hadn't. The thing was, he was woefully inept. Everything he said came out wrong, his words tumbling into the air like half-dead flies that were annoying and all you wanted to do was swat them away.

He blurted out, "Where's Colonel?"

"In his bed." And back to the book.

"What are you reading?"

No answer. Was that a blush that crept up over her cheek? Clearly flustered, she blinked furiously.

"Nothing."

Henry watched her, sized up the profile. Her nose. That nose was so small and flat, she hardly had one. What would happen if he told her that?

All summer long, she had been a kind of torment; he realized that now. All he wanted to do was look at her, to get her attention somehow. Nothing worked.

He wanted to snatch the book, slam it to the swing, grab her by the shoulders and make her look at him, to really look into his eyes and notice that he was there.

But what he did was get to his feet, wish her a good night, waiting for her answer the whole way across the porch and through the kitchen door.

Now here he was, fishing half-heartedly, watching the field lane for any sign of her. He knew it was futile, but still he watched.

Finally, he gave up, took the last bluegill off the hook, flipped it back into the pond, and watched it swim away into the deep blue-green depth, wishing he could free himself from his attachment to Anna. Hooked. He was hooked. He grinned wryly, bent to close his tackle box, picked it up with one hand, threw the rod over his shoulder, and walked away from the pond.

Verdant growth was all around him. Summer rains and blazing sun had produced heavy, dark-green stalks of corn, a veritable forest of it, growing ten feet tall, already pushing large yellow ears. The alfalfa was a vast rippling sea of short, round-leafed grasses, with a hint of lavender blooms.

Third cutting would be necessary soon, but already the bays were full on each side of the barn. Walnut trees sprouted the cluster of young walnuts forming along their branches; the chestnuts would produce clumps of burrs, the prickly outer coverings that housed the fragrant chestnut. Pumpkin vines were hip high, small lime-green pumpkins already forming beneath them.

God was blessing Lancaster County's rich, brown soil for yet another summer. He was an amazing, benevolent father who so richly gave mankind all things to enjoy.

So, Henry thought, after all my prayers, there is always God's love, His presence surrounding me. His ways so far above my own that I can't even begin to decipher them. So I will trust, cast all my cares upon him, and lean not to my own understanding.

Perhaps Anna was not the one God intended for him. Perhaps he was meant to be alone on his journey of life on earth, only to be reunited with Harvey some glad day when his own walk of life was over.

Who could know?

There would always be unexpected twists and turns on life's pathway. The important thing was to meet each new bend in the road with faith and courage.

All these thoughts spun through his head like a stiff whirlwind, the kind that appeared out of thin air on a sultry summer day and displaced corn stalks or leaves or dust, anything in its path.

Courage he did not have. That was the only sure thing.

Deep in thought, he was jerked back to reality by a high keening sound, followed by a series of yelps that traveled up and down the scales from pain to terror and back again, a cadence that sent chills up Henry's spine.

He dropped his tackle box and fishing rod and took off running in the direction of the sound. He followed the field lane where it made a Y; to the left led to buildings on the farm; to the right led through a maze of corn and alfalfa, then to woods bordering the property.

As he neared the woods, he realized twilight had already fallen, so he would find the wooded area even darker.

The yelping ceased for a moment, then resumed. He followed the sound to the dark form of Colonel, who was down on his stomach, turning his head from side to side, trying to rid himself of the hateful quills embedded in his face. A porcupine! Poor Colonel had tangled with the dreaded creature that protected itself by loosening these barbed quills of misery into a prying dog's nose.

He dropped to his knees, talking all the while. The yelps faded to whimpers as Henry stroked the suffering dog's back.

Where was Anna?

Nowhere in the woods. So he'd have to get the dog back to the house for a pair of pliers, by the look of things.

Henry stood up. "C'mon. Come here, Colonel."

He snapped his fingers, wheedled, coaxed, and did everything he knew to get a dog to move, with no response.

Exasperated, Henry tried lifting him, but quickly set the dog back on the ground after the series of yelps started up again. Well, there was only one sensible thing to do, and that was to leave him and go get the pliers and Anna.

He found the tool he needed on the workbench in the shop, lit a lantern in the milk house, then went to the house for Anna, who had already gone upstairs.

He called her name.

She appeared on top of the stairs, her face registering nothing.

"Your dog tried to get acquainted with a porcupine. He's crying and setting up an awful howling in the woods. I need you to come with me."

"Be right down."

By the time he retrieved the lantern, she was there, her eyes on his face.

"What happened? I thought he was in bed."

"Evidently not."

"Where were you that you heard him?"

"Fishing."

She had to run to keep up with his long, swift strides, her skirt swishing about her legs, her bare feet flying across the grass of the field lane.

The lantern bobbed up and down.

They heard the dog's yelps before they found him. Anna fell to her knees, murmuring to herself or the dog, Henry couldn't be sure, then lifted her face to Henry.

"There's a whole bunch of them. What are we going to do? How do we get them out?"

"Pliers."

She put a hand over her mouth, wide-eyed, as Henry knelt, held the dog's face to the ground, clamped the pliers on one end of the long, hollow quill, and pulled.

Nothing.

Colonel must have known this was the only way to rid himself of the awful quills, so he stayed quiet;

only his eyes spoke of the agony surrounding his nose and face.

Henry attached the pliers again, and yanked. He was rewarded with a quill clenched firmly in the mouth of the pliers. Anna held the lantern, without speaking, while Henry worked in the damp heat of the woods, until every quill had been safely removed.

Colonel sprang up, then bent his forelegs to rub his face in the soft moss and moist earth on the forest floor.

He emitted all kinds of strange noises.

Anna laughed outright.

Henry laughed with her.

"Poor thing, he must have suffered terribly."

"He did, sure. Look at this." Henry picked up a quill to show her the barbed end that had been embedded in the dog's face. "A dog never makes the same mistake twice."

"I believe it. These quills are like fishhooks, really."

"Smaller hooks, but yes, they are. Is that why you don't go fishing?" Henry asked, looking down at her in the glow of the lantern.

"No." Anna pondered his question for a long while, then took the plunge. "I didn't learn to fish because you liked Katie."

Henry became very still.

He could hear the chirping of the robins calling their children to bed, the chirring of an excited squirrel, and knew this was the perfect chance. Like nature, like the ways of the woods and God's creatures, it was time.

So he said, "I did. I loved Katie, but she was not God's will for me. He took her away."

Henry stood openmouthed with surprise, watching Anna take off, like a bird in flight, her bare feet making no sound, distancing herself from Henry with every step, Colonel bounding by her side.

He clutched the lantern in one hand, the pliers in the other, and followed slowly, shaking his head.

Well, chalk one up for speaking at the wrong time, sticking my foot in my mouth, ruining everything once again. I don't talk at all, then when I do, it's out of time.

Ah, better to forget all of it. Women were something he would never understand. Better that he stay single. Didn't the Bible say it was better to stay single, for some? When a man married, he cared for and loved his wife, taking away that single-minded service to the Lord.

The minute he stepped into the forebay, all that rational, spiritual thinking went right out the door. There she sat, weeping softly, her dog's head in her lap, swabbing at the wounds with an antiseptic solution dissolved in a bowl of warm water.

Henry's heart was touched beyond any restraint.

He dropped to his knees, set the lantern to the side, and placed a hand on her small shoulder.

"Don't cry, Anna. He'll be all right."

Anna sniffed, but continued swabbing at the torn spots.

"He's suffering terribly," she whimpered.

"Not like he would be if we'd have left them in there."

"You're right. But isn't there an easier way to remove them?"

"I have a feeling the veterinarian would have done basically the same."

She looked up at him. The porcelain sheen of her skin with an underlying blush beneath her cheek made him take away his hand. It had a mind of its own, and he wanted to touch her cheek to see if it was real.

But of course, after that first bumble, never, never.

"Do you want me to stay here with you?"

"Oh, you need your sleep, Henry."

What was this?

She thought only of him, of his comfort, and agreed with his point of view about the dog. It all came as naturally as breathing. And this tender weeping?

"I'll stay here with you," Henry said, softly.

The only answer was the hiss of the lantern, an occasional rattle of the chains attached to the Belgian's halters when they dragged them up over the wooden trough to reach for another mouthful of hay. Somewhere, a cow lowed quietly. From the shadows, a yellow barn cat appeared, curious, then melted back into the night.

Anna kept the dog's head in her lap, stroking, easing the pain with her soft words.

Finally, Henry spoke.

"I spent a lot of time out here, with Lucky, after Harvey died."

"I know."

"Yeah, I guess you do. You were here."

"I missed Harvey. He was nice to me."

"He was nice to everyone."

"You both were. You know, Henry, I've often thought many boys like you don't turn out well. They feel misplaced after they spend their years growing up with another family."

"Yes, I can understand that. But it's hard growing up with your real family if you know the weight of poverty. I mean, we were happy; children usually are, even in dire circumstances. But you finally come to see where it was for the best. My father was never a happy man. I never told anyone my whole life, but I overheard my parents more than once, from the register cut into the kitchen ceiling. It was the grate to allow heat to circulate upstairs, and if you knelt there, it was like being in the same room with them. I can still hear the . . . I don't know. He was saying how often he doesn't want to continue with life, how easy it would be to leave this earth, and, well . . ."

Henry's voice faded away.

Anna's eyes became large and frightened.

"He wouldn't have taken his own life?" she whispered.

Henry shook his head.

"These things are not talked about, Anna. You know that. It is a shameful subject. They don't have funerals for someone who does that. But I'm not sure he wasn't tempted. He may have tried something at one point. My stepmother . . . well, there's no use talking about it now."

"But isn't it a condition? Something wrong, if a person feels like that?"

"My sister used to say it was the devil."

"We don't know, do we? It is sad, when someone like your father suffers from a feeling of hopelessness."

"I think, although I was only a young boy, I always knew there was something wrong with my father. He told us many times it was only a matter of days before Hitler's army would storm Lancaster County, and we'd all be taken to Germany."

"You believed that?"

"Sometimes."

"But that was an awful weight for a young boy."

"Harvey and I were close. We assured each other that it wasn't going to happen. And it didn't."

She looked down at the injured dog, gently pushed him off her lap, and began to rise.

"You should go in, it's getting late," she said.

"Think Colonel will be all right?" Henry asked.

"I think so. He's tired. He'll sleep."

Together, they rose, walked to the house.

The night was still, and the humidity clung to the night air. Henry smelled the roses that grew in profusion up the post at the edge of the porch. He dreaded going inside, to the stuffy upstairs bedroom that held the heat like a thermos bottle.

"Let's sit here on the swing for a while," he said.

She said nothing, but made her way to the swing and sat at the farthest corner. Henry took up the opposite side, shoved softly to put the swing in motion. Heat lightning rippled across the dark sky.

"Anna, why did you run off when I mentioned Katie?"

"I don't know."

"Tell me."

"No."

"Please?"

She hesitated. He could see her small hands pleating the folds of her dress, restlessly searching for a purpose.

"I don't know," she said again.

"Did I say something wrong?" he asked gently.

"No."

"What is it, Anna?"

She took a deep breath. "It's just that I spent so much of my life wondering if you loved Katie, and when you said you did, it was really hard, I guess."

"Why?"

"Don't ask that question."

"Is it because you cared about me?"

"I always cared about you. You were my brother."

"*Ach*, Anna, I'm not your brother."

Henry strained to hear her words, but he knew she said them, so he hesitated, unsure how he would answer.

"It would be better if you were," she said.

Now what did she mean by that? Confused, Henry didn't know what would be the proper response. Afraid to open his mouth, Henry looked out toward the barn, the night deepening around them.

Finally, he asked. "How would that be better?"

"Just better, I guess."

"You're not being clear."

"All right, I'll tell you what I mean. I have always been the quiet one, the one who was in the background. My sisters have always overshadowed me, especially where you were concerned."

"But. . ." Henry floundered.

"No, let me finish. Growing up together, my devotion to you and Harvey bordered on worship. But Katie was the one you noticed. She was better at everything. Remember the skates you received that first year? Remember how it was Katie, not Malinda, who taught you how to fly across the ice? It was always like that."

Suddenly, Anna placed a hand on his arm.

"Why did you never ask Katie to be your girlfriend?"

"I wanted to. Just never could summon enough courage. She was so much more than me. Of course, it hurt when she began dating. But, I don't know, perhaps it wasn't meant to be. Do you think God controls all matters of the heart?"

"That's a tough one. Obviously, people get married for all the wrong reasons, and spend a lifetime of mostly being unhappy. So you think, 'They made that choice; they brought it on themselves.'

"Or did they? I believe God allows everything to happen, for a higher purpose, in so many ways we don't understand. We can't figure it all out by ourselves, so we do the best we can, from day to day."

Henry nodded.

He was deeply touched by Anna's wisdom, for a young girl who had always lived a sheltered life on the farm.

"If I were to say that I wanted to begin dating you, would that mean I would have to move?" he asked, his heartbeat accelerating to the point where he was sure he would slide off the porch swing in a faint.

"Are you thinking you might say that?" Anna asked.

"Well, that all depends on what *your* thoughts might be on the subject."

He actually was frightened now; the possibility of hyperventilation or fainting loomed ahead. He knew he could not move from this swing without asking her if she was interested in him, but was hopelessly mired down in the bog of pretense.

All he had meant to do was test the waters, like sticking a finger in a pot of liquid heating on the stove, and he found himself unable to tell her he was serious.

What untold agony was this courage, or lack of it!

Anna, in her kindness and wisdom, reached across the great divide and spoke gently.

"If we are becoming more than a brother and sister, which I believe is happening, then yes, you will no longer be able to live here with us. The ministry will never allow it, neither will our parents. So let's both pray about it, and let God lead the way."

Henry nodded in the dark, opened his mouth to say kind, appropriate words of agreement, but there were no words, only a long intake of life-giving breath.

# Chapter Nine

IT WASN'T LONG BEFORE BOTH EPHRAIM AND Rachel became aware of the budding romance that played out right under their noses. Till the autumn winds blew, Ephraim helped Henry inquire about renting the old Tom Adams place close to Gordonville. He also gave Henry a team of horses and a sizable loan to begin raising hogs and chickens, and to start up a small dairy.

The farm was everything Henry had ever dreamed of. Where the road took a turn down a steep hill, then to the right, the Pequea Creek was wide, close to Rohrer's mill. The drive that led to the farm turned left, after you passed the mill, nestled between two hills, with woods on either side, set back from the buildings far enough to frame them with a curtain of gold, red, and orange.

The house was small, built in the traditional two-story "cracker box" farmhouse style, its narrow porch built by someone whose top priority was frugality. The absence of a *kesslehaus* was no big deal, as long as Henry lived there alone, he'd do his laundry on the porch.

Sparsely furnished with leftovers of Rachel's and some dishes Malinda brought packed with newspaper in a cardboard box. He had a cast iron frying pan, a blue agate coffee pot, a good hunting knife, and a potato masher.

The wooden panes on the windows were falling apart, some of the pieces of glass missing, so Ephraim taught him how to repair windows with penny nails, panes of glass, and putty.

The barn housed the horses at one end and cows at the other. There was no real cow stable, no cement stanchions, and certainly no gutter, so Henry cleaned the cow stable every day without complaint. It was more important to save every dollar toward a cow stable and more cows than to have everything handy.

The small barn was built into a hillside, called a bank barn, allowing the horses and wagons to pull hay and straw into the second story without a problem. It was sturdy, built with good timbers, attached to each other by round, wooden pegs. There were remnants of feed sacks, drifts of old hay, corncobs, and rusted equipment covered with thick spiderwebs like lace handkerchiefs draped over everything.

Nothing deterred Henry.

He awoke before four o'clock every morning, milked five cows by hand, strained and cooled the milk in galvanized cans, set it in the cold water or a mechanical cooler, then cleaned the cow stable, fed the six young hogs and twenty-four chickens.

He worked till late in the evening, cooked a pot of bacon and beans, or corn mush, washed it down with homemade root beer or ginger ale, and went to bed.

He tilled the fields, sowed fall oats, and hauled manure under lowering November skies, dreams of the future taking up most of his waking hours, thinking of the time when he would bring home his lovely bride, Anna.

He often shook his head, muttered to himself, and even laughed. If someone could have observed him bouncing along on the harrow, they might seriously think of having his sanity checked by a good doctor.

It was all so unbelievable, so incongruous, the way his life was taking shape, everything falling into place like building a brick wall. Much more than he deserved.

Or didn't he?

His thoughts infused by a heady glow, past sorrows and trials swam away to a forgotten recess of his heart. The lid on the small aluminum stockpot had to be pressed down on all the dollar bills that accumulated there. Almost enough to put in the cement work of a decent cow stable or another cow. The chickens were still laying good for November. A young gilt was about to give birth. He asked Abner Beiler for one of his golden retrievers as soon as Betsy had her pups.

Ten dollars, he said.

It was too much, but Henry missed the companionship of a good dog. Nothing would ever replace Lucky, no dog or horse or cat, but he missed the sight of a good dog rising from his bed of straw in the morning, come to greet him with the affable waving of a plumelike tail.

He built a new chimney, with Ephraim's help. He had pronounced the old one unsafe, saying it was better to spend the money to replace it than lose the house some cold, windy day.

Henry felt capable, basked in Ephraim's praise, soaked up his girlfriend's adoration, and went to bed feeling blessed, thankful for all the talents and gifts God had bestowed on him.

All he remembered when he woke in the predawn darkness of the frigid bedroom was the undeniable thought that there was something wrong, something terribly amiss.

His mouth had gone dry as sandpaper, his eyes wide, staring into the now-hostile dark, the inky void filled with heart-stopping portent. His heart hammered like a frightened bird in his chest, his thoughts exploded like sparks, igniting a fear the likes of which he had never known.

He felt as if he might lose his mind. He had to get out of bed, to do something, but he was so consumed by dread that he thought the floor might open and he'd fall through it.

He took a deep breath, inhaled sharply, then exhaled slowly. He did it again.

He tried to pray, to summon God's presence, but his words seemed to go no farther than the plaster ceiling above him.

He tried to steady himself, to wait and take stock of this odd happening.

Like a flash, it all came back to him.

A dream.

A vivid dream, in which the Pequea Creek had risen, brown and turbulent and muddy, roiling along, laughing at him in an evil fashion. He stood rooted to the bridge, much taller than he actually was, the wind roaring, pushing at his back with a fierce power. He knew he would topple into this laughing, beckoning water if he didn't stop growing taller, but he had no power to keep this from happening.

Then he saw Harvey, crying out for help. But it wasn't really Harvey; it was Anna.

His precious, beloved Anna.

He cried out, into the darkness surrounding him, more afraid than he had ever been.

Dear God, please tell me. The only answer was the suffocating darkness, rife with unanswered questions.

He spoke to Anna, he told Ephraim. They both assured him it was only a dream. Likely he had overworked himself and was tired out, having done without good nutritious meals for too long.

"Don't put any stock in dreams," Ephraim said.

"They are *fer-fearish*," Anna said.

Rachel cooked a roast of beef, made lima beans and potatoes with the skins on, for their vitamin and mineral content. She gave him a bottle of cod liver oil to take, and chamomile tea.

He may as well have chewed on a raw fish as taken the disgusting cod liver oil. He left the tea in the brown paper bag and never touched it.

The thing was, he didn't believe what Anna and her family told him. He had a deep inner conviction, an unspoken need to find out what God was trying to say. Hadn't He spoken to men of old? Look at Samuel in the temple. Called over and over when he was a young innocent boy.

The snow came the first week of December. At first, soft fat flakes came down and melted on the brown grass, but the temperature dropped, the wind picked up, and the fat flakes mixed with icy pellets that rattled against the barn windows as Henry forked hay to the cows.

He wished he'd brought more wood in from the woods. It was unlike him, this lethargic feeling that drew sleepy cotton over his eyes in the morning. He had no appetite, so he opened a can of beans and ate them cold, standing against the white metal sink, one foot crossed over the other, shedding straw and manure, still wearing his barn coat.

The dream was a harassment. It took away his peaceful days, his energy, and his bright-eyed eagerness for the future. He plodded about, distracted, doubtful. He jumped at the slightest provocation. His face turned pale, his eyes sunken.

Anna became alarmed, that Sunday evening in December. They were sitting at the kitchen table, drinking coffee, toying with the sugar cookies Anna had brought out on a pretty platter. Normally, Henry would have consumed three or four of them immediately.

"Henry," Anna said, her eyes dark with worry, "can't you tell me what is troubling you?"

Henry shook his head.

"If I would know, I would tell you. I don't know."

"Is it still that dream?"

"No. Yes."

Anna looked at him in disbelief.

"It still bothers you."

"Yes, it does."

"But you know my parents and I don't believe God talks to us through dreams."

Henry lifted agonized eyes to her face. "But it was so real, Anna. It's infused into my senses, and I can't shake it. I think about it all the time."

"That is a weakness, Henry. You must rise above it."

"I disagree."

There, he finally had the courage to stand on his own two feet. Not to belittle her, or argue with her, but to voice his own opinion on an extremely important matter. Yes, he was only Henry, but he had a right to say what he believed in.

They parted that evening with a polite handshake, an air of disagreement tempered by Anna's wisdom and quiet demeanor. They had agreed on the kind of courtship that would include no physical affection. Anna felt very strongly there was a special blessing in this, to remain chaste and pure before marriage.

At first, Henry had been hurt and angry, wondering what was wrong with an occasional hug or a kiss. Everyone did it, but he respected Anna's views, adopted them as his own, and looked forward to the day when they would be married.

It was that night, a few days before Christmas, when Henry was woken from a sound sleep. There was no fear, no dry-mouthed terror, only the knowledge that he was fully awake, the darkness around him cold, but pleasant. It was a friendly darkness, a darkness that gave its approval of him.

And then, like a soft sigh scented with every imaginable flower that grew all over the world, he understood the dream. As soft as the falling of a spent rose petal, the releasing of a daisy's white flower drifting to the ground, his mind was instilled with the sweetness of what God wanted him to know.

He had grown too high in his own eyes. God had work for him to do, someday, somehow. It was so simple, so sweet and reassuring.

He never told Anna. He just resumed his vitality and his plans for the future, but gave all the honor to God, and not to himself.

Christmas dinner was held on New Year's Day that year, everyone bowing to Malinda's wishes. Her husband's family had too many dinners and Christmas singings going on, and she couldn't take it. She was only one person, and she couldn't take all the clothes *rishting*, the washing, getting the children off to school on time, before preparing for yet another event.

Their family was growing with a new baby at regular intervals. Malinda being in charge, things went well on a daily basis. But when the holidays rolled around, the Christmas spirit was hard for her to grasp.

Henry drove in to the home farm, the sun glinting off the silver barn roof, the snow like a sparkling pristine blanket of white, every pine and bare bough coated with a layer of fluffy snow.

The sun shone, the air was still, life was beautiful for Henry. God was everywhere for him these winter days. He felt the presence, which was drawn closer by the gratitude that came from a heart filled with praise. He felt he had been rescued from going down the slippery path of self-honor, when everything unfolded just the way he wanted.

So there was a spring in his step, a healthy flush to his cheeks, a glad light in his eyes when Anna surprised him at the door of the forebay.

"Hello, Anna!"

"Hi, yourself."

"You're not in the house?"

"No actually, I had this Christmas present to take care of. I think he's a little more than I can handle."

Henry led his horse to a stall, tied him, and hurried out to see what she meant.

Sure enough, a brown ball of fluff, a golden retriever puppy, wriggled into her arms from Lucky's doghouse. Anna scooped him up, held him so tightly he grunted, her face breaking into a picture of pure delight.

She giggled as the dog licked her face. "You name him," she said, smiling up at her future husband.

Colonel trotted into the barn, stopped, and sat on his haunches, gazing up at the new puppy with the weirdest expression.

"Jealous, aren't you?" Anna chortled, bending to hold the puppy to Colonel, allowing him to sniff him all over and become acquainted.

Henry watched her, fascinated with her lack of fear and her understanding of Colonel's personality. He wasn't sure he would have held the puppy to the large German shepherd quite as freely, but Colonel seemed to accept and even welcome the newcomer.

"You sure have a way with dogs, Anna."

She straightened, held the puppy to her shoulder, then smiled at him.

"You're serious?"

"I am. I'm not sure I would have trusted Colonel."

"Oh, he's all right. He would never hurt the puppy. Most dogs are very social, only the ones who are mistreated have a problem."

"But, didn't you say Colonel was?"

"Sometime, yes. But he seems to have outgrown it."

"Hopefully," Henry said.

Normally Henry would not have been invited to the Christmas dinner if he was dating Anna, as courting was kept a secret, mostly, in the 1940s. But Rachel felt differently, saying Henry was their son, and Anna a daughter, so of course, he would be present.

They did not acknowledge each other throughout the day. Henry visited with the men in *die gute schtupp*, while Anna stayed with the women.

Besides Malinda and her rowdy crew, there was Uncle Levi King, Ephraim's brother, Abner Beiler and his wife, Rachel's sister Lydia, plus dozens of nieces, nephews, and cousins.

Outside, the snow fell softly, hushed by the lack of wind, the flakes drifting down to cover tree branches and bushes, the graveled driveway, and the brown grass in the yard. The men's hats were dusted with soggy snowflakes, melting as they stomped into the *kesslehaus*.

The kitchen window was propped open with a small piece of trim, steam rolling from the vast kettle of boiled potatoes, Rachel shaking in a teaspoon of salt, while her sister-in-law wielded the potato masher, her round, gold-framed spectacles steamed, obscuring her view. She yanked them down, peered over the top to continue stomping the potato masher up and down with a certain fury. Behind her, little Rachel and Lydia watched, fascinated, at the jiggling of her hips, the flapping of her big arms.

Henry sat with the men, a cup of strong black coffee at his elbow, his long legs stretched out before him. He was content to take no part in the conversation, just sit in the warmth of the house and absorb the news, the latest prices from the New Holland auction barn, the price of feeder pigs, and the accident on Route 340.

He sat up and took notice when Uncle Levi described the latest design in hay balers, wondering how long until these wonderful pieces of equipment would become widespread, easily available, or *alaupt* by the Amish church.

Uncle Levi was known as a progressive, unafraid to voice his rather strident opinions, but an interesting warmhearted chap whom Henry had always liked and admired deeply.

He watched Abner Beiler pick up a fat little girl, as cherubic as an angel, smile down into her face, and hold her on his knee. She leaned back against her father, her bright brown eyes like two polished stones, wedged between the fold of soft baby fat on her cheeks.

Henry smiled at her.

She turned her face and buried it in the folds of her father's vest, then peeped out at him a few seconds later.

Henry smiled again.

He felt a stab of joy. This was exactly what he wanted, a life belonging to a group of people who were like-minded and dwelt together in unity and love.

Mostly.

He wanted to raise a family, on a farm, his own farm, repeating the cycle of the seasons, over and over, his Anna by his side, supporting him in his work. He hoped he would not expect too much of her; he knew Amish housewives worked hard and shouldered responsibility much more than he had any idea. Anna was so small, so petite, somehow he felt a need to protect her and help her with life's burdens.

She was so childlike, so trusting of him.

Henry sat in the living room that Christmas Day, his last one as a single young man, emotions spilling from him, through him, in ways he could not always comprehend.

Like the horn of plenty, the cornucopia of assorted fruits and vegetables, the bounty of earth's plenty, so he savored this living room, a haven of Christmas comfort and joy. The apple of a grateful heart, the clump of grapes his safekeeping through the years of difficulty, the oranges and carrots, the fleshy, glossy green peppers and red-cheeked tomatoes. He lifted each one, examined the gifts the Lord had so kindly bestowed on his life.

Rachel and Ephraim.

Anna, the most dear.

Even Harvey's death, and Katie's. Each one a stepping stone on the way to maturity and a closer walk with God. His own sad father, also a gift, though perhaps a bitter one, to understand each time he also felt downhearted without reason. He was, after all, his father's son.

Anna gave the dog the dubious name of Buford.

"Why Buford?" Henry asked.

"Look at his eyes. He just looks like a Buford. Buford Esh."

She giggled, snuggled the brown, doe-eyed puppy to her face, and sighed contentedly.

He had never loved her more.

The seasons came and went. Till November of the following year, the Ephraim King farm had been cleaned and painted, scrubbed and washed, so every available surface was sparkling clean for Henry and Anna's upcoming wedding.

The trees were bare by the end of that month, except for a few scraggly brown oak leaves that clung to the branches extended over the porch roof, like a clean-shaven face with a few skipped bristles.

Rachel had a fit about them.

She worried about all of them letting loose and falling on the yard and sidewalks the morning of the wedding. She was no sloppy *hausfrau* and never would be, and she had no intention of being one now.

Ephraim made fun of his perturbed wife. But he watched good-naturedly from the barn as Henry set a ladder against the porch roof, climbed up with a feedbag, pulled those leaves off, stuffed them in the bag, and climbed back down.

Rachel told Anna she was, indeed, marrying a winner. Any man that bowed to a woman's foolish whim was worth praising.

Anna smiled her secretive little smile but chose to keep her thoughts to herself.

It rained on their wedding day, November 24, and turned to ice before the service was over. But the gas lamps hung from their hooks in the ceiling sputtered cozily, and the warm air was permeated with the rich smell of chicken filling and mashed potatoes. An uncle who had been a bishop for many years preached the sermon. Each word that fell from his lips was inscribed on Henry's heart. He took all the old stories very seriously, especially that Adam was lonely in the Garden of Eden, and God created a beautiful woman for him to be his friend, his partner, his lifelong companion.

It was so simple but so true.

Henry had experienced that himself. Everything had gone so well for him on the rented farm he called his own, and still there was an element missing, a piece of the puzzle incomplete. After today, the house would be filled with the essence of a woman, the one for whom he had waited so long.

As was the custom, Henry and Anna did not move to the farm till March. It was an old tradition, to allow the young groom time to prepare his home, while the bride stayed with her parents, sewing, preparing quilts, hooking rugs, crocheting doilies and pillowcases, and so on.

They visited the home of every guest who had been at their wedding. In below-freezing temperatures with billows of snow borne on the harsh winds of winter, they traveled from one corner of Lancaster County to another, visiting people, collecting the *haus schtire*, the wedding gift.

None had been brought to the wedding. The gifts were withheld until the *yung-Kyatte* came for a sumptuous meal. Newlyweds were highly esteemed, the visit considered a great honor, the table loaded down with many home-canned or home-cured delicacies.

After the meal, they would sit in *die gute schtup* and hold lively conversations while Anna produced a canvas top, with different colors of yarn to be pulled through, creating a unique pattern of flowers, or a design of tulips to be sewed for a pillow top that would be placed on the cane-seated rocking chair in Henry and Anna's *gute schtup*.

When it was time to leave, the hosts would proudly bring a shovel or rake, perhaps a heavy wrench or sharp saw for Henry, a blue agate canner or a sturdy potato masher or a stainless steel bucket for Anna.

As Henry went to hitch up the horse, Anna shrugged into her heavy black coat, pinned the black shawl snugly around her shoulders, took off the white covering and placed it in a small, overnight suitcase, her *coppa-box*, donned a heavy woolen headscarf, and placed the homemade black bonnet on top. Over her face, she wore a thin black scarf, wound around and around, leaving only a narrow opening for her eyes. After she pulled on heavy gloves, she was prepared for the long ride in the roofless, one-seated courting buggy.

Her feet encased in large rubber boots, bricks heated in the oven and wrapped in towels, she stayed half-warm, as long as the distance was not over ten miles.

There were times, however, when the distance was closer to twenty, and that was when Anna's teeth clacked together uncontrollably, like castanets, her body shivering with the cold, and her feet were like blocks of ice.

These were the times that tested her endurance, her strength, and the much-touted submission to her husband.

# Chapter Ten

IN MARCH, THE GLAD DAY FINALLY ARRIVED.

Ephraim and Rachel deemed it was well and good that Anna would be a proper *hausfrau*.

The wind whipped the women's skirts to one side and sent the men's hats rolling across the yard. The horses' manes blew off their arched necks, whipped to the opposite side, their tails streaming to the same direction. They pranced, champed at the bit, made many false starts, halted by irritated movers with a loud, "Whoa! Ho there, Fred."

The wind was only a minor annoyance.

Henry laughed as cardboard boxes wobbled across the yard, slammed drunkenly up against the fence. He ran after wildly flapping pieces of newspaper, securing them with a chaotic churning of his arms and legs.

Nothing could alter his high spirits. Nothing.

The wind was harsh, yes, but the buds were pushing on the trees, the spring peepers had sounded down by the creek, that high, shrill call of lonely males doing their best to attract a mate.

The red-winged blackbirds had arrived, showing the trimmed red wing as they took flight, calling out the beloved, "Birdie-glee, birdie-glee!"

Henry knew the moist soil would be loaded with nitrogen from the heavy load of winter's snow. The roots and stems of winter wheat were pushing, as was the new seeding of alfalfa.

Anna received a new table, made by deacon Amos Esh, and four chairs from the Mennonite named Abel Horning.

They were sturdy, well-made chairs, with acorns and oak leaves painted on the back.

They were given an icebox, a used Servel, painted blue, one Aunt Lydia had in her *kesslhaus* for years. It worked well, and for twenty dollars, you just couldn't beat it.

After they all wended their way down the winding driveway, Henry and Anna sat side by side on the new davenport, surveyed their house, with satisfaction, a sense of awe.

"Somebody pinch me," Anna murmured, laying her head on Henry's shoulder.

He drew her close.

"I'm relieved to hear you say that, Anna. I was so afraid you'd miss your mother the first evening."

"Oh, my, Henry. I've waited for this moment for so long."

Before going to bed, Henry got the *Gebet büchly* from the desk top, and looked at Anna with a question in his eyes.

"You planned on saying the *gebet* together, as we've taught our whole life?"

She nodded, a small smile on her lips, her eyes filled with trust.

They knelt side by side, in front of individual kitchen chairs as Henry opened the book to a German evening prayer. He read fluently the words written by men of old, in a low well-modulated voice that carried well.

Anna shivered, chills creeping up her spine. It was if he had been reading German prayers all his life, and with a women's intuition, she knew.

She pondered all this, her heart accepting what her mind did not.

Henry was special. He had suffered more than some much-older folks, and suffered well, without self-pity or drawing attention to himself. Anna knew that he valued his walk with God even above his love for her.

She smiled a small, secretive smile. She would see what she could do about that.

That spring, life was poignantly sweet for the young couple, their days filled with rewarding hard work, their evenings spent sharing their innermost thoughts, dreams, and hopes.

Henry was prone to continued conversation, now that his beloved Anna sat by his side, listening, nodding her head, occasionally adding a word of correction, or one of wisdom.

As the days grew warmer and the evenings longer, Colonel and Buford would join them on the porch, splayed out, their tongues lolling as they wound down from the day's activities.

Buford had grown into a beautiful, silk-haired retriever with the fine curtain of silky hairs on his underside and down the back of his legs. He had taken second place to the alpha Colonel, who had established himself as Buford's guardian when he was a puppy.

Colonel walked over and rested his head on Anna's knee. Crickets chirped beneath the wooden floor of the porch. A barn cat slunk around the corner of the well house at the end of the sidewalk. The barn rose up beside the driveway, peeling red paint hanging in shreds from graying boards like blisters. Behind the barn, the ridge showed brilliant shades of new green, small purple Judas trees flecked among them like lace.

The field lane wound up behind the barn, a narrow, brown track that led to the back thirty acres. Robins dived through the air, clumsy with haste, calling raucously to their wide-mouthed babies that huddled hungrily in their nest.

Henry pushed Buford aside to get up and go to the kitchen for a drink. Buford lifted his head, blinked, then lowered it on his paws.

Anna watched Henry go.

The one and only sadness of her life was that he had never really accepted Buford or Colonel. Outwardly, he put on a good show, but she knew he would never love these dogs the way he had loved Lucky.

Henry was not aware that Anna saw through the thin veneer of his pretense. Oh, he liked the dogs; he just didn't love them. She would come to accept this in time, and she was determined to never let him know how she felt.

In time, Henry gave his patient wife a detailed account of his companionship with Lucky. The dog had been like a sponge, a soft, warm, silky recipient of all his grief, tears, and loneliness.

Lucky understood human suffering in a way other dogs did not. Henry had spent hours brushing the silky long hair, seated on a bale of straw, before he went to school.

He told Anna that when he cried, Lucky felt his pain, the way he laid his heavy head on his knee and looked straight into his face as the tears puddled in his eyes, then ran over, down his cheeks and off his chin, sometimes dropping on Lucky's head.

"You see, Lucky was baptized by my tears. He was a special dog sent from God. I don't doubt that one instant. When Lucky showed up in that snowy field, God already knew he would replace Harvey. So he was a miracle."

Anna listened, drying a stainless-steel saucepan at the sink, her towel going round and round. Henry was seated at the kitchen table, with the last of his coffee growing cold in the cup, the way it often did.

"But you do like the two dogs we have now?"

"I do. Oh, of course, Anna. But they're not Lucky."

"I know. I notice things."

"What?"

"Well, you just don't enjoy them the way you enjoyed Lucky."

"Yes. Yes, I do. The farm would be so empty without either one. Especially Buford."

Anna nodded, smiled, and the subject was finished.

She was very wise, her womanly intuition right on the mark, more often than not. It was something Henry would always hold in high esteem, the way she sensed his moods. Indeed, she was a woman worthy of his praise.

She kept an immaculate house and garden, took on her share of the milking, and helped Henry in the fields whenever he needed her. Every day, Henry thanked God for his lovely wife, their health and happiness, and the ability to serve Him.

When their first baby was born the following year, they named him Ephraim, after Henry's adoptive father, and Anna's.

He was a scrawny, red-faced little fellow, with a shock of light hair like long peach fuzz. He was like a starved bird, his mouth always open, his yells of outrage powered by an extraordinary set of lungs. Like bellows, they were.

Henry tried his level best to be a patient, understanding husband, hovering over poor Anna and her squalling infant in anxiety, wanting to clap his hands over his ears and run out the back field lane to get as far away from these frightening screams as he could.

"Your milk has no food value," Rachel said.

"He's hungry," Aunt Lavina said.

"His stomach hurts," Mattie said.

"Paregoric," Daddy Beiler said.

Definitely chamomile. Peppermint. Catnip. Goat's milk.

Hold the baby upside down.

Bewildered, Henry milked all the cows while Anna stayed in bed for ten days, then dressed and rested on the sofa or a rocking chair.

Uncle Levi's Rebecca came to stay, a mild-mannered sixteen-year-old with no experience and a stilted aversion to dogs and men.

When told she would be expected to help with the milking, she told them politely, her words laced with steel, that she never milked a cow in her life and she had no intention of starting now.

Henry ate burnt eggs. How could you burn an egg? They were actually charred.

He washed them down with scalding cups of tea, ate the white bread she served instead of toast, and charred sausages that were pink everywhere but the outside.

He never said anything but was always kind, praising her ability to manage the washing and ironing. But he was met with a hostile stare and her feet planted firmly with toes to the side like an ostrich.

Wasn't the birth of a baby a joyous event, one that tied the bonds even firmer, love multiplied by three? What had gone so wrong?

Anna seemed foreign, far away, dark circles under her eyes, going about her days grimly, the shouts from the baby increasing as weeks turned into months.

Where was the relief? Where was the joy?

But as these things go (as Rachel soothed and held and patted and encouraged), it only lasted for a while. With a smile on her face, she told them, "This, too, shall pass." And it did.

By the time Baby Ephraim was six months old, he was a chubby, rosy-cheeked boy who ate anything they fed him with seemingly no ill effects from the contracting stomach pains or the lungs that had been used to the limit.

Anna smiled and laughed and swept up her baby, kissing him from the top of his head to his toes. Henry found out about the joy and love of babies. It had just been delayed for a while as little Ephraim worked through bouts of colic.

A few years later, Levi was born, a solemn-looking child who weighed two pounds more than their firstborn. He slept all night and most of the day. Ephraim toddled around and stuck his finger in the sleeping baby's eye, or pulled on the thatch of brown hair and said, "*Ich gleich net ihn.*"

Henry laughed, received the full amount of joy, and praised God every day for the miracle of babies. He told Anna they'd have a dozen more if they were all like Levi.

Anna beamed. Her blue eyes shone into her husband's adoring gaze. She said she would love to have many more babies, until their table was filled with children.

"Blessed is the man whose quiver is full," Henry quoted, while Anna nodded in agreement.

And then, old Solomon King passed away at the age of seventy-nine. A leader of the Gordonville district, a *diener zum buch*, he was mourned by everyone. He was a pillar in the church, a staunch supporter in time of need, a powerful speaker who never failed to lay wisdom on hearts. The church prospered beneath his tutelage.

There was talk of ordaining a minister to take Sol's place, but no one took it too seriously, least of all Henry and Anna.

They were too young, they assured themselves.

A year later, an announcement was made. In communion services, they would ordain a minister.

Votes were taken, and five men were in the lot, Henry among them. He was the chosen one, selected by God from the five. Henry bowed his head and felt completely undone, inadequate, and unable.

They drove home in near silence, Anna's hand resting on his forearm, without saying a word. After the flurry of well-wishers had gone, they spent a sleepless night, alternately praying and crying, talking and holding each other while the boys slept peacefully, unaware that their father had been ordained a minister.

Their family grew again, with the birth of baby Rachel. Henry walked into church services with the ministers and the deacon, learned to preach in the manner of the Amish, and read German scripture with ease.

They bought the farm, built a cow stable, and milked ten cows by hand. The fields produced abundantly, and the mortgage dwindled as each year passed.

Ephraim and Levi, at the ages of ten and twelve, could help with chores now. Two more boys had been born after Rachel, Enos and Harvey, then Anna.

Four boys and two girls in all.

The years were kind to Henry and Anna. They worked hard, enjoyed the children, and spent many days together, working side by side.

Colonel and Buford were both old and stiff, but close companions to all the children, a constant sight around the farm.

When Henry was ordained bishop, the family accepted their lot with grace, bowed their heads, and asked for wisdom to lead the church.

Henry was a gifted speaker, well known throughout Lancaster County. He had known sorrow and pain, had sympathy for the suffering and the poor in spirit.

Harvey's death seemed a far-away memory.

How could he ever have thought of Katie, when Anna was so obviously the perfect helpmeet?

God's ways were fascinating, his love beyond comprehension. Henry grew in spirit and kindness and love.

Anna's days were blessed beyond measure.

When Christmas came that winter, Anna bought another Newfoundland puppy from a dealer. They hid the large, floppy dog away for two days, until Christmas Eve.

They waited until Henry was in his study, his German scripture and his copy of the German and English dictionary open on his desk, his head resting on his hand, his eyes half-closed as he struggled to stay awake.

He heard the scraping, the tittering and giggling, before the door burst open, and shouts of "Merry Christmas, Dat!" erupted from all the children, grouped around a cardboard box, with Anna in the background.

"My, what is going on here? A surprise? A Christmas surprise?"

They jumped up and down, and squealed and shouted. Into the chaos, Henry dived, laughing, pulling off the top of the cardboard box to find a bored-looking miniature Lucky sitting in the middle, his small, triangular brown eyes quizzical, as if to say, "Why were you making all this fuss?"

Henry was completely taken by surprise. He didn't know there was a black Newfoundland to be found for hundreds of miles. The children watched wide-eyed as

Henry lifted the puppy, held him to his face, then sat with him on his lap, stroking the silky hairs, reminiscing, remembering those years with Lucky.

His eyes filled with tears.

"Thank you, everyone. You thought of the perfect Christmas gift."

When Henry was ordained bishop of the north Gordonville district, he felt the weight and responsibility without an ounce of strength. Drained, confused, unable to see his way, the path too steep and too rocky, he groaned from his innermost soul, begging God to be by his side, show him the way, and he would not lean to his own understanding.

But he had Lucky now. A gift from his children and his beloved Anna. And from God.

The years passed, with Henry growing in spirit.

His beard was streaked with gray, his wavy hair thinning, but he was still a stalwart figure, tall, wide, with an arresting face.

What was it about that face, people thought.

They listened, rapt, as he preached in his kind, compassionate way. He visited the sick, spoke words that were meaningful, and was held in high esteem by the members of his congregation.

He often returned to that night of terror, the dream like an unspeakable dragon, the meaning crystal clear as he traveled through life as a minister, and then, *da full dienscht.*

To God goes the honor. All good and perfect gifts come from above, from the Father of lights. Love for Anna grew in ways beyond his imagining. On her forty-second birthday, their last child was born, making an even dozen. A daughter named Mary.

All the children gathered round his table, and he could honestly say his quiver was full.

Seven sons and five daughters.

Each one brought up by Anna's quiet discipline, her everlasting patience and love. If the children did well, he gave his wife all the credit. And he still loved Lucky, padding around the well-kept farm in his funny rolling gait, the loose skin with the abundant silky black hair, the only kind of dog that would ever touch his heart.

He often knelt in the haymow, away from prying eyes, clasped his hands, and prayed for God's wisdom, His strength and guidance, with Lucky sitting by his side, listening to the sound of his master's voice.

Side by side, just the way he sat with Harvey as a small boy, given to the Ephraim King family.

Side by side.

## The End

# Glossary

*Alaubt*—Allowed.
*Boova*—Boys.
*Chackets*—Jackets.
*Da full dienscht*—Bishop.
*Da mon*—The man.
*Dat*—Dad.
*Denke*—Thanks.
*Die boova sinn do*—The boys are here.
*Die glany boovy*—The little boys.
*Die gute schtup*—The good room, i.e., the living room.
*Diener zum buch*—Minister.
*Die schveshta*—Sister.
*Eisa kessle*—Iron kettle.
*Fer-fearish*—Misleading.
*Fliesichy boova*—Ambitious boys.
*Gebet buch*—Prayer book.
*Gebet büchly*—Small prayer book.
*Glauk*—Complaint.
*Gluck*—A sitting hen.
*Grischtag essa*—Christmas dinner.
*Grischt Kindly*—Christ Child.
*Guta Marya, boova*—Good morning, boys.
*Gute boova*—Good boys.
*Hausfrau*—Housewife.

*Haus schtire*—Wedding gift.

*Hesslich hinna-noch*—Behind schedule.

*Huddlich*—Messy; chaos.

*Ich gleich net ihn*—I don't like him.

*Kesslehaus*—Washhouse.

*Knecht*—Hired hand.

*Komma*—To come.

*Kommet*—Come here.

*Mit die fuhr*—With the team, i.e., horse and buggy.

*Müde binnich*—A German evening or bedtime prayer for children.

*Ponhaus*—Scrapple.

*Rishting*—Preparing

*Roasht*—Chicken filling.

*Schem dich*—You should be ashamed.

*Schoene boova*—Nice boys.

*Schpinna hoodla*—Spider webs.

*Ordnung*—Literally, "ordinary," or "discipline." The Amish community's agreed-upon rules for living, based upon their understanding of the Bible, particularly the New Testament. The *Ordnung* varies some from community to community, often reflecting the leaders' preferences and the local traditions and historical practices.

*Vassa droke*—Water trough.

*Vella essa*—Let's eat.

*Vell. Voss hen ma gado?*—Well, how did we do?

*Youngie*—The youth.

*Yung-Kyatte*—Newlywed.

*Ztzvilling*—Twins.

# OTHER BOOKS BY
# LINDA BYLER

## LIZZIE SEARCHES FOR LOVE SERIES

BOOK ONE       BOOK TWO       BOOK THREE

## SADIE'S MONTANA SERIES

BOOK ONE

BOOK TWO

BOOK THREE

TRILOGY

# LANCASTER BURNING SERIES

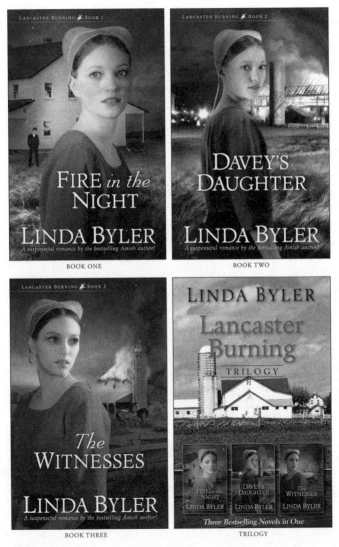

LANCASTER BURNING ✦ BOOK 1

FIRE *in the* NIGHT

LINDA BYLER

*A suspenseful romance by the bestselling Amish author!*

BOOK ONE

LANCASTER BURNING ✦ BOOK 2

DAVEY'S DAUGHTER

LINDA BYLER

*A suspenseful romance by the bestselling Amish author!*

BOOK TWO

LANCASTER BURNING ✦ BOOK 3

*The* WITNESSES

LINDA BYLER

*A suspenseful romance by the bestselling Amish author!*

BOOK THREE

LINDA BYLER

Lancaster Burning

TRILOGY

FIRE *in the* NIGHT
LINDA BYLER

DAVEY'S DAUGHTER
LINDA BYLER

*The* WITNESSES
LINDA BYLER

**Three Bestselling Novels in One**

TRILOGY

# HESTER'S HUNT FOR HOME SERIES

BOOK ONE

BOOK TWO

BOOK THREE

TRILOGY

# The Dakota Series

**BOOK ONE**

**BOOK TWO**

**BOOK THREE**

**TRILOGY**

# THE LONG ROAD HOME

BOOK ONE

COMING SOON

BOOK TWO

COMING SOON

BOOK THREE

AMISH CHRISTMAS ROMANCE COLLECTION

AMISH ROMANCE AT CHRISTMASTIME

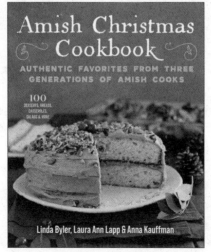

AMISH CHRISTMAS COOKBOOK

# CHRISTMAS NOVELLAS

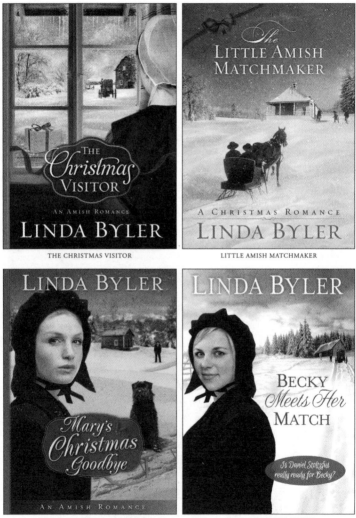

THE CHRISTMAS VISITOR

LITTLE AMISH MATCHMAKER

MARY'S CHRISTMAS GOODBYE

BECKY MEETS HER MATCH

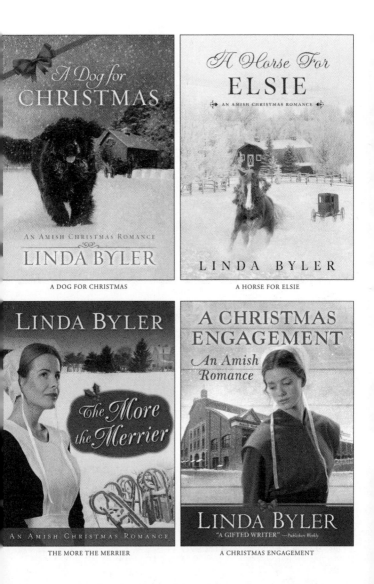

A DOG FOR CHRISTMAS

A HORSE FOR ELSIE

THE MORE THE MERRIER

A CHRISTMAS ENGAGEMENT

THE HEALING

A SECOND CHANCE

HOPE DEFERRED

LOVE IN UNLIKELY PLACES

# BUGGY SPOKE SERIES FOR YOUNG READERS

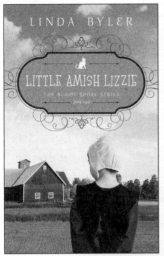

BOOK ONE

BOOK TWO

BOOK THREE

# About the Author

LINDA BYLER WAS RAISED IN AN AMISH family and is an active member of the Amish church today. Growing up, Linda loved to read and write. In fact, she still does. Linda is well known within the Amish community as a columnist for a weekly Amish newspaper.

Linda is the author of five series of novels, all set among the Amish communities of North America: Lizzie Searches for Love, Sadie's Montana, Lancaster Burning, Hester's Hunt for Home, and The Dakota Series. Linda has also written four Christmas romances set among the Amish: *Mary's Christmas Goodbye*, *The Christmas Visitor*, *The Little Amish Matchmaker*, and *Becky Meets Her Match*. Linda has co-authored *Lizzie's Amish Cookbook: Favorite Recipes from Three Generations of Amish Cooks!*